The Roads We Must Travel

Short Stories
by Jeffrey Miller

ISBN: 978-1-945917-03-5

Printed in the United States of America

Cover Design: Chris Reilley
Front Cover: *Painting of a Night Street with Colorful Lights* by Grandfailure
Edited by: The Fussy Librarian Editing Services

Also by Jeffrey Miller:
Invaders from Mars and Other Tales of Youthful Angst
Damaged Goods
War Remains
Waking Up in the Land of the Morning Calm
Ice Cream Headache
When a Hard Rain Falls
The Panama Affair

Big Table Publishing Company
Boston, MA
www.bigtablepublishing.com

Grateful acknowledgment is made to the editors of these publications in which the following stories appeared, sometimes in different form:

Blue Hour Magazine: "Going After Sexton"
Drunk Monkeys: "The Roads We Must Travel"
Foliate Oak: "Wind Chill Factor"
In Between Altered States: "What Happens in Vegas Stays in Vegas"
    (Originally published as "Wedding Night")
Literally Stories: "Black Roses"
Literary Yard: "For Emily"
Notes Magazine: "Mojave Green"
Stirfry Literary Magazine/Damaged Goods: "As Long as I Have My Cokes
    and Smokes"
Story Shack: "Killing Geckos"
The Linnet's Wing: "Rain on Me"
The Literary Nest: "Papa Was a Rolling Stone" (Originally published as
    "Just Like a Rolling Stone")
Veteran's Voices: "Maid-Rite"

"Mojave Green" and "Going After Sexton" originally appeared in *Response Time*, Western Illinois University, 1989 as part of the author's MA thesis; "Black Roses" originally appeared in Eureka College's literary magazine, *Impressions*, 1987; parts of "Yuki no Sasayaki" appeared in *Short, Fast and Deadly* as "Thicker than Blood."

Acknowledgements

I would like to extend my heartfelt gratitude to my publisher, Robin Stratton, for her guidance, support, and friendship over the years. I am deeply indebted to her and the Big Table Publishing Company for making this book a reality.

And finally, my love and gratitude to my wife, Chiu, and our four lovely children for all their love, support, and understanding.

For Forrest Robinson, Loren Logsdon, and John Mann;
my mentors and literary guiding lights

Table of Contents

As Long as I Have My Cokes and Smokes

"As long as I have my Cokes and smokes."

This is what you tell me on the Number 9 bus on a cold, rainy November day as the bus winds through narrow streets toward downtown Hamamatsu.

It smacks more of a mantra than any earthly desire for caffeine or nicotine. You say it nonchalantly as if it is an afterthought, a stream-of-consciousness utterance. I wait for you to finish your musing, but it hangs there in the damp air and then, trails off into silence.

On a condensation-beaded window, I practice my Japanese writing skills. I count each stroke in my mind as I guide my finger across the cool surface and draw the Japanese character for Hamamatsu. I find comfort in how everything—even the Chinese characters I don't understand—has a symbol and meaning.

Six months ago, I couldn't even read these Chinese characters which the Japanese call Kanji. Now, I know that the Kanji for *hama* means beach and the Kanji for *matsu* means pine tree. Pine tree by the beach. It could be the beginning of a poem; it should be the beginning of a poem, but I haven't found the time to jot down a single line of verse.

The night we found out we had been hired, we split a bottle of wine from the bargain bin at Sonny's Liquors and looked forward to all the poetry we would compose.

"I'll be the Pound to your Snyder," I said, clinking our glasses together.

Nine months later, we are still waiting for the inspiration, though time had run out.

Two more strokes and I finish this Kanji, for Hamamatsu. It reminds me of a toilet seat exploding next to a tree; my Kanji doesn't cut it and has already started to run as the condensation drips down the window. I wipe the window and my sloppy Kanji clean. I wish I could start over.

"Excuse me?" I ask. "What's that supposed to mean?"

11

"You're not even listening to me," you stammer. Your bottom lip quivers. "You never listen to me anymore."

An elderly couple sitting to our left has been eyeing us ever since they got on the bus two stops after we did. We're probably the only two foreigners they've come across all week. I can just imagine them thinking *gaijin*. In Japanese, *gaijin* means foreigner. It sounds so visceral when I've heard it uttered in my direction. I wonder how it sounds when it is thought.

Cokes and smokes? I shake my head. When did we get on this topic?

We started this conversation at breakfast, continued it in the staff car to the Suzuki Headquarters for our morning company classes, and now, on the bus six hours later, pick up where we had left off in the morning. I suppose it's appropriate that no one knows what we're talking about. Frankly, I don't know what we're fighting about. I think it might be about how you don't like me always changing my mind at the last minute, like last weekend when we were going to ride this cute little red single-car train into the country. I said that we could ride the train any old time and should go to Hamamatsu Castle instead because it was such a beautiful autumn day. Little things like that, I guess. You used to like my spontaneity.

Then again, we've been drifting apart ever since we arrived here.

Three schoolchildren in bright yellow raincoats and yellow plastic helmets board the bus, grabbing a ticket from a vending machine, and sit down behind us, giggling. *Kawaii desu ne*. Cute.

When you get on the bus, you take a ticket from a machine that indicates your fare zone; on a display board above the driver, you know exactly how much you will need to pay based on your destination. Everything is calculated and preordained. Nothing left to chance. I look away and gaze at the floor; I can't get over how clean the inside of the bus is—even on a rainy day.

"So, this is it, then?"

You twist the ring on your finger and look out the rain-streaked windows. "I don't know."

12

Japan, as it turned out, wasn't what either one of us expected. Six months ago, it all seemed so exotic and mysterious. However, the Orient wasn't as strong and alluring as we led ourselves to believe. Now, we both have to find excuses to finish our contract and stay together.

I gaze at the floor again. Once I saw a 500-yen coin in the middle of the aisle on the Number 9 headed downtown. I watched people gaze at the same coin as they boarded and exited the bus and no one stopped to pick it up. That coin wouldn't last a second back home in Chicago. When I had mentioned this to one of my colleagues, Martin, he told me that in Japan, no one would pick it up because it didn't belong to them.

"Then it would just lie there and no one would get it," I said.

Martin nodded. "That's the whole point, my friend. No one wants to upset the yin and yang."

Of course, eventually, someone would *have* to pick it up, but I did appreciate, for that moment, the cosmic significance of that coin.

I hold your left hand. This has already gone too far, and we might not be able to turn back. You turn and look at me before you stare out the window as the bus nears a Shinto shrine. In the reflection, I already see the tears and mascara running. From our apartment to the bus terminal downtown, there were nine shrines. The same number of the bus we rode on now.

"Bill's going to go through the roof when he finds out," I reply. Bill was our boss. He was from New York and had been childhood friends with Robert De Niro. He always made a point of bringing that up whenever he talked about how much he missed the old neighborhood. *Bob and I did this. Bob and I did that.* It was amusing at first until we found out that they hadn't been *too* good of friends. They lived on the same block. One thing that hadn't been amusing was when Bill found out that we weren't married. "He's probably going to fire the both of us."

I think about everything that we would have to do if we were forced to leave. Classes would have to be shuffled and canceled.

Money would have to be returned. Tickets would have to be bought. At least we wouldn't have to divvy up too many of our things; we didn't have too much to begin with.

"I don't know," I continue, turning to you. "Maybe we could give it another try."

You furrow your brow.

"Us. I mean us."

"It's too late."

That's when you bite down on your bottom lip, the way you always do when you've already made up your mind about something. This conversation, like the rain falling, is fleeting in the grander scheme of things.

The bus slows as it passes the shrine; from here, it's a straight shot downtown. The first time we rode the Number 9, we got off at the wrong bus stop and spent the rest of a rainy summer afternoon exploring narrow streets lined with old antique shops and teahouses. With our *Lonely Planet* phrase book in hand, we navigated our way through that day, running in and out of shops to get out of the rain, much to the puzzlement of shopkeepers.

We discovered the coolest record store and the quaintest teahouse that afternoon, and later, inebriated by the sweet, earthy smell of freshly installed *tatami* back in our apartment, made love on the new futon we had bought that day.

One of the three schoolchildren, who has been fidgeting in the seat behind us ever since she noticed the two *gaijin* sitting in front of her, finally decides to try out her limited English on us. You and I both know the drill.

"Hello," she says, giggling. "How are you?"

I look at you and smile, but you continue to stare out the window. *How are you? If only you knew, kid.*

Three stops later, I decide to get off and have some noodles. I remember this hole-in-the-wall noodle shop run by an elderly Taiwanese couple, one of the shops we had stumbled across that rainy summer day.

14

"I'll call you later." I walk toward the front of the bus as it slows down. I turn and look back, hoping for some sign, any sign, but the elderly couple, also getting off, has blocked my view. I count out my fare of 100 and 20-yen coins, dropping each one with a syncopated clang, and clatter into the metal fare box.

Before the bus pulls away, I look at you through the window as the rain streams down it in rivulets. I hope again for a sign, a glimpse; however, you do not turn. You just look straight ahead.

I hear your words, *as long as I have my Cokes and smokes* once more inside my head until I can't see the bus anymore. Then I remember where I heard that before. It was a couple of weeks after we arrived, and we were riding downtown for a class in the Press Tower, next to Hamamatsu Station. It was one of those days that all we go through sooner or later: when the littlest culture bumps begin to wear you down. You were upset about something. Maybe it was the way that some Japanese women stared at your tall frame or how the clerk at the Entetsu Supermarket who always giggled at us whenever we checked out. You turned me to me then and said that as long as you had your Cokes and smokes, everything would be okay.

I pull up the collar of my blazer, stick a damp cigarette into my mouth, and head toward the noodle shop tucked away between a *pachinko* parlor and a coffeehouse. One steaming bowl of noodles and cup of green tea later, it's back to our five-tatami mat room and cold, empty futon, but first I remember to pick up some smokes.

What Happens in Vegas Stays in Vegas

Two weeks after I'd met Suzy in the parking lot of the Cocky Bull, we were in my buddy's Impala headed north across the eerie moonscape-like desert to Las Vegas to get married.

My family back in Illinois didn't know. In my mind, I could hear my mother demanding to know how I could marry someone two weeks after we met in a bar, and my father trying to calm her down: "Well, he is twenty-one now."

My buddies warned me about her, but what did they know? It wasn't like they were going to talk me out of marrying the girl of my dreams. There she was, slow dancing in front of the band playing "Tequila Sunrise" while drinking one. I didn't care much for the band, some Eagles wannabe, but I did like the song and the way Suzy moved. And boy could she move. Later, when I found out she had come to the Cocky Bull with another man, it made the night all the more special. A pity for him; lucky for me.

After I finished the graveyard shift at the air base outside of Victorville and borrowed a suit from one of the guys in the barracks (as well as smoking a big, fat joint with him—his wedding present), Suzy, and her two friends, Billy and Joy, and I were off to Vegas. We spent the morning waiting in line at the Clark County Courthouse for our wedding license. Some people couldn't wait to tie the knot. The couple in front of us, who met the night before at a casino, got married by a judge just minutes after they had their license.

Choosing a church, once we had our license in hand came the fun part. Suzy had her heart set on the Silver Bell Wedding Chapel as soon as she laid eyes on it. For starters, it really did look like a chapel—this white clapboard building with what appeared to be stained-glass windows and a steeple, surrounded by the cutest white picket fence you could imagine (though, the red and yellow neon sign out front and neon trim around the eaves were a bit over the top). I wanted to get married by the King at the Graceland Wedding Chapel—how could anyone *not* want to be married by an Elvis impersonator? However,

Suzy protested. Billy and Joy lent us some money so we could have the deluxe wedding that came with photos, a cassette recording of the vows, and a bouquet of daisies. The package also included four tickets to a show, casino tokens, and a complimentary bottle of champagne.

The minister, reverend, or whatever religious moniker he used to sanctify the vows reeked of whiskey and cheap cigars. Halfway through the "ceremony" he launched into a drunken ramble about how he grew up not far from my childhood town and had only come to Vegas to get a new lease on life. Then, when the ceremony was over, he asked me for a tip, or a donation to the church, as he put it.

The show turned out to be some off-the-strip venue, but the guy that played Chuck Campbell, the ventriloquist with his dummy Bob on TV's *Soap*, headlined along with a chorus line of naked women dancing to the music of *Star Wars* as they brandished illuminated plastic light sabers, which looked more like giant dildoes than a Jedi's trusted ancient weapon of choice. Suzy quaffed most of the champagne and promptly ordered more, followed by shots of tequila and bottles of Coors. Then she started on the tequila sunrises. She sure could put them away. When she fell off her chair for the second time, that was our cue to leave.

Outside, while I waited for Billy to bring the car around, a hooker propositioned me, but as soon as she saw Joy and Suzy staggering out of the casino toward me, she smiled and shrugged before sashaying down the sidewalk. Out of the corner of my eye, I saw our "minister" putting his hard-earned fees to good use with her. He looked in my direction and smiled, before the two of them drove off in his blue convertible.

We had the $3.95 all-you-can-eat buffet special at the Circus Circus resort before we went back to our motel located next to the airport. As soon as we arrived back at the $12.95-a-night motel, which came with a complimentary bottle of cheap bubbly and more tokens for one of the casinos, Suzy made a beeline for the bathroom. I stripped down to my shorts, fed some quarters into the vibrating bed, and turned on the television just in time for *Saturday Night Live*.

"Suzy, are you okay?" I asked.

She said something unintelligible, which I took for, "I am so sick," as she vomited into the toilet.

Eric Idle was the host of *SNL*, and Kate Bush was the musical act. Idle's monologue was pretty funny. I heard Suzy retching again in the bathroom. I cracked open a Bud and reached for the phone. On the other end, Dad answered, though he wasn't too happy to have been woken up.

"It's me, Ray," I said, swigging the beer. "Yeah, I know what time it is. I just wanted to let you and Mom know that I got married today."

It got quiet on the other end, and I heard him wake my mother. Through two time zones of static, I heard the two of them yelling. First, he yelled that I was old enough and then she yelled that I was his son and that this would have never happened if he would have spent more time with me as a child. As I listened to the two of them arguing about who was more responsible for my upbringing, I went through Suzy's purse on the nightstand. There was a small pistol and a tube of ointment. *Apply three times a day*. I knew about the pistol but not the vaginal infection.

After my parents had finished debating their parenting skills, my father came back on and told me how happy he and Mom were for me. In retrospect, I probably should have given them a heads up.

I heard Suzy vomit again.

"Oh God, please don't let me throw up anymore," she mumbled as she flushed the toilet again. She never could handle her tequila sunrises.

Finally, my parents got around to asking how we were.

Outside, another jet took off, rattling the windows.

"We couldn't be happier."

Papa Was a Rolling Stone

My father met the Rolling Stones somewhere on the road, the year he ran away from us.

I found out thirty years later while my brother, Danny, and I were cleaning our grandmother's house shortly after she passed away. The radio was playing oldies, and a Stones song came on. Danny grinned and said, "Every time I hear them, I think about Dad meeting them."

I dropped the garbage bag I was filling. "Wait a minute. He met the Rolling Stones?"

Danny rolled his eyes. "I'm surprised he didn't tell you."

I picked up the garbage bag, tied it, and threw it into a corner. "Dad didn't tell me a lot of things, Danny." Dust danced in a ray of sunlight as the bag landed near a window.

"Oh. Well, he met them on a bus and rode a long ways with them, to Oklahoma I think."

"Come on," I said, quickly changing the subject. "Let's get this crap out of here."

His trip out West—now, that was something that I *did* know about. It was not long after he had taken me fishing, and told me—right there on the banks of the Illinois River—how he would be going away for a very long time. To a ten-year-old, a very long time was somewhere between lunch and supper and supper and breakfast.

This was just right after he had helped me reel in what turned out to be a five-pound catfish.

"I got it, Daddy! I got it, Daddy," I said excitedly.

"Careful, son," my father coached patiently. "You don't want to reel in too fast."

"Okay, Daddy."

He stood behind me and ever so carefully, so as not to damage my confidence, took hold of the pole and helped me reel in the fish. Together we watched it flapping around, mouth and gills gasping, at the end of the line.

19

"That's a good one, son," my father said as he put his arm on my shoulder.

He had made some peanut butter and jelly sandwiches, wrapped in waxed paper; he handed me one, but I wasn't hungry. They were too warm and soggy. After that I could never eat a peanut butter and jelly sandwich again.

"When are you coming back, Daddy?" I blinked back the tears.

"I don't know, son," he said. "Not for a while."

Years later, that trip out West turned out to be a story told and retold when everyone got together for the holidays, usually after too many drinks, and usually after some coaxing from one of his brothers. There we were—uncles, aunts, cousins, nephews and nieces, Grandma and Grandpa—sitting around the decimated holiday turkey, vestiges of cold yams in coagulated puddles of giblet gravy, and a melting Jell-O fruit ring when he launched into the "story."

Except, there was never any mention of the Rolling Stones.

"It was just outside of Flagstaff," my father began, popping open a can of Hamm's. "I was out of money and hadn't eaten since Tulsa."

The amount of embellishment was proportional to how much or how little he had drunk that year. One year he described how he hadn't eaten since St. Louis. Another year, he threw in that he stole an apple pie cooling on the windowsill of a farmhouse he passed on the outskirts of Rolla, Missouri. Well, not actually stolen, my father added. He left a note with his address in Illinois and the promise that he would send the money once he found work. I think that might have been some scene he saw in a movie and tailored for his story.

"I had crossed this field when I thought I heard singing. It started out low and got louder the more I walked. Like a beacon. It echoed off the mountains and rolled across the desert. Well, I followed this melody wherever it was coming from. And there it was—this small church in the middle of the desert. It was Sunday morning. That choir's singing was the most beautiful music I'd ever heard. I walked inside and sat in the back and fell asleep."

20

Probably drunk someone snorted, followed by laughter.

"After the service, I met the preacher and his wife and told them that I had gone out West to look for work," my father said. "They invited me to their home, gave me something to eat, and offered a bed to sleep in that night. I was so tired I slept until the next day."

Those expecting a more dramatic ending might have been a little disappointed with what followed next.

"The next day I called home," my father continued, "and Dad wired me the bus fare. I was on the next bus home."

End of story.

There were a few groans and sighs before someone turned on the football or basketball game. If it hadn't been my father who had run away, it might have been a good story. Perhaps, the kind of story that we could have laughed about over a couple of beers.

It wasn't entirely my father's fault, though, for never talking about the time he met the Rolling Stones or caught a line drive foul ball off the bat of Ernie Banks at Wrigley Field. They were not the kind of stories he could bring up when we did get together during his monthly visits.

No, I never recalled him talking about anything out of the ordinary. With Mom sitting in the kitchen and listening in on the conversations we had with our father, he kept it simple. His repertoire of questions was relegated to asking about school and what we wanted for our birthdays.

Before he came over, though, my mother coached Danny and me what to say and what not to say. The few times that he managed to get us out of the house alone, he was generally quiet.

He always dressed up when he came over; a nice pair of slacks and shirt. Even when he lost his job at Caterpillar, he still made sure to at least make a good impression during those monthly visits.

Then there were all those awkward Christmas mornings when he came over to pick us up to take us over to our grandparents' house; the birthdays that he remembered; the occasional camping or fishing trip that was meant to fill in for all the parenting he had missed. We went through the motions of being father and sons. I think Danny was lucky. He was too little to remember.

Dad never knew what to say, even then. I suppose we never knew what to say, either. When we got back home, though, Mom asked us what he had said, which was usually followed with, "Did he give you any money?"

What I remembered most, though, was him leaving. That much had been ingrained in my young, impressionable mind I guess. He used the excuse of going fishing to get me alone so he could tell me that he was leaving and that he might not be back for a long time.

Later, my father and I were just friends. I went into the Army. We had our beers when I was on leave. "Hey, everyone, this is my son. He's in the Army." Then, after I got out of college, we had our beers again. "Hey, everyone, my son just graduated. A round of beers on me." Of course, he hadn't given me a dime. Still, I let him celebrate.

Over the years, we still saw each other around the holidays if I was in town. There were still the birthday cards or phone calls and later email to stay in touch. But by then we had drifted so far apart that not even the Stones could have saved us.

Danny and I had the onerous task of going through most of the stuff that our grandmother had collected over the years—stuff she picked up on all the trips she took with our grandfather—no doubt despite his constant protestations that it was, after all, just junk.

"Probably made in China," he would murmur with a hint of sarcasm in his voice. His most famous utterance to anything he felt was inferior.

Dad didn't have the heart to tell Grandpa Pete, who had recently taken up residence at the Prairie View Nursing Home, that he had to sell the house. I remembered Grandpa Pete always going on and on about how he had worked his whole life for the house and how happy he was on the day in 1970 when he finally paid his last mortgage payment. Now, he was going to lose it without even knowing about it.

Grandma's medical bills had drained his bank account and had started to draw on my dad's.

When his two older brothers couldn't help out, everything fell on my father's shoulders, and it started to wear him down.

I could see that Dad was in a foul mood when he pulled up in the truck he borrowed from a buddy to haul everything to the landfill. He was coming back for the fourth trip now, and with each additional trip, his mood soured. Most of the stuff that had not been carted off to the landfill was going to be put in storage; the rest burned.

"You guys about done?" he asked, getting out of the truck.

"Yeah, we just have to haul some more stuff out of the living room," Danny said. "We got everything out of the basement like you asked."

"We've got to finish today," our father said, puffing on the last of a cigar. "I've got a guy from Century 21 looking at the house tomorrow. He says he's already got someone lined up to buy the house."

One thing my father and I agreed on was that we hated to see the house go. My father had grown up in the one-story, prefab house Grandpa Pete built in 1946 and I spent many summers there. All through elementary school, as soon as school ended in June, my grandparents would pick me up and I would stay until the beginning of August. However, the house was just too much for my grandfather to take care of, especially after having a minor stroke a few years ago.

"I want to get this stuff down to the landfill before it closes," my father said, tossing another bag of garbage into the back of the truck. "I think one more trip ought to do it. The rest of it…we can burn in the back. You want to have some beer and chicken later?"

Danny said he had to get back to Chicago.

I had nothing else to do.

"Sure," I said.

"How come you never told me that you met the Rolling Stones?"

After my father had taken the last load to the landfill, we met up at the Rainbow Tap about a mile down the road. We were on our second beer and waiting for our chicken dinners: a quarter dark with a side of fries, salad, and a chunk of Vallero's Italian bread. Three guys seated at the bar were watching some bowling tournament. We had a table off to the side, close to the kitchen.

"What?"

"The Rolling Stones. How come you never told me you met them? Danny said you met them when you were out West."

My father furrowed his brow as he thought hard for a moment, trying to remember something he hadn't thought about in years. "Oh yeah, the Rolling Stones. Why are you bringing this up now?"

"We heard one of their songs on the radio this afternoon, and Danny said that you had met them. I just wondered why you never mentioned it to me."

"Just never crossed my mind, I guess."

"You told Danny."

I watched my father shake some salt into his beer, something he learned from Grandpa Pete, and watched the foam rise in the glass. I wasn't quite sure about the science behind this beer trick. It was fun to watch, though.

"It would've been cool to know that my old man met the Rolling Stones," I said.

"We just talked. They asked where I was going and—" He stopped mid-sentence and gestured to the bartender for another round. "I wanted to know what they were doing in America. One of them had a guitar and played a song. I had no idea who they were until years later when I saw them on *The Ed Sullivan Show*."

"It's not like you only met them. You practically partied with them." I took a drink of beer. If I had known this bit of information when I was in college, I would have been a god. "You know, all those times you told the story about when you went out West, you never brought it up."

"It was nothing, really."

"It might have been something to me," I said.

My father stared at me from across the table. He raised his hand, as if to point at me, but then grabbed his beer. He shook his head and took a drink. He was too tired to get into it over the Stones.

I was not about to let him off too easy, though. There was still one question—that *one* question—that I had always wanted to ask him. Maybe it was not the best time to bring it up, but this was just as good a time as any. Suddenly, I was that ten-year-old on the banks of the Illinois River and, this time, I wanted to know. "Why did you run away from us?"

There, I finally said it; but I should have chosen my words more wisely. My father glared at me and rubbed his chiseled chin. Someone dropped a metal pan in the kitchen. We both looked in the direction of the kitchen and then turned back to the table.

Then my father sighed deeply as he leaned forward, placing both arms on the table. "I was out of work and running out of choices. I needed some time to think," he said. "Maybe that wasn't the right thing to do at the time, especially when I had you boys to think about. I thought if I could get a good job, your mom would want to take me back."

"Why did you have to go all the way out to Arizona to find a job? It seemed more like you just wanted to get away from everything."

My father stared at his beer and then looked up at me. The past two months had been rough on him with Grandma Loretta passing away, and having to put Grandpa Pete in a nursing home.

"You're right, I did run away. It was wrong, I know, but I came back ready to patch things up," he continued. "The same day I got back home, I called your mom and wanted to meet her."

I studied my father's face. All those years I never really looked at my father closely. Most of the photos I had of him were of a younger man. Now, he looked so tired.

"She wanted nothing to do with me," he said. "I tried, but I guess we were just different. We were too young when we got married, and I suppose we both fooled ourselves into believing that we could ever patch things up."

My mother, known more for her stubbornness than her openness, especially when someone crossed her, never talked much about why she divorced Dad, but for years, the bitterness she had in her heart for him ate at her more than the cancer did. She could be mean and unforgiving when she wanted. My father never stood a chance.

"You know, all those times when I came over, it really hurt me that I could only see you once a month or on holidays," he said slowly. "One time, not long after the divorce, I was late sending her the support check, so I decided to bring it over. She wasn't home—you and your brother were at your grandparents' house at the time—but I spotted her car outside Buddy's Tap. I was foolish to go in there, but I was worried more about what she would do if she didn't have the check on time.

"She was in there all right, at the far end of the bar sitting with two guys, Don Woodshank and Lester Jackson. When I tried to give her the check, she told me—" My father stopped and was silent for a few seconds. "Let's just say it wasn't too nice. She threw the check back at me. I left and the next day, I put the check in the mail like I should have in the first place. Two days later, I got a call from her attorney threatening to haul me back to court for being late with the check."

Funny how, when I'd waited so long to finally hear my father's side of the story, it made me feel sad for him. To think he had kept this inside of him all these years. And if it hadn't been for the Stones, I probably would have never known.

My father was silent for a few minutes as he stared at the beer in front of him. "You know, I never knew my real father."

I wasn't ready for that revelation.

"I wish I could have known who he was." He stopped and took a drink of his beer. "Your grandpa was a good father. He took very good care of Mother—your grandmother—and me."

As a kid, I was always curious about why my father's last name was different than his brothers'. Of all the things my father and I did talk about in later years—when I was old enough to know better—the two things we never talked about were the divorce, and the fact he was adopted.

From what I pieced together over the years, my grandmother's first husband had run out on her when my father was just a baby. He probably couldn't handle having to take care of one more baby during the Depression. Though my father's older brothers went to stay with an aunt, Grandpa Pete adopted my father not long after he had married my grandmother, just a couple of months after World War II ended. My father never knew his real father.

One Christmas, when I was fifteen, I had asked my father why his last name was different from my uncles' last names.

"It's a long story," he had said.

Just like his trip out West, I had thought at the time and left it at that.

Now, I wasn't going to let him off the hook. What we should have talked about years ago was finally going to see the light of day.

"Did Uncle Bob or Uncle Ray ever talk about him?"

"It was just one of those things we never discussed, just like why your mom and I got divorced. I was just a child when your grandmother finally divorced him," he said, "probably no older than you were when your mom and I got divorced."

We ordered another round of beers and another plate of chicken and fries. The bowling tournament was replaced by some fishing show. Two men were casting their lines from a boat in the middle of a lake hemmed in by towering pines with snow-capped mountains in the background.

"When hauling in his northern pike," echoed the voice-over narration. *"Brad realized that his line was about to snap."*

"Oh, he's going to get away," yelled Brad from the television.

"Steady, Brad. Just reel it in slowly."

My dad, an avid fisherman himself, had momentarily gotten caught up in Brad's struggle with the pike. He shook his head and muttered, "Tsk, tsk" when it appeared that the fish was going to get away.

"Amateurs," he mumbled and turned back to me.

"So what did you find out?" I asked.

"I made a few inquiries here and there, located a distant cousin," my father said slowly. "He wasn't a bad man. He just made some mistakes, and that is why your grandmother divorced him. He died a few years after that. Your grandmother married your grandpa Pete, and life went on. I don't know why I waited so long to find out about him, but then what would it have changed?"

I tore off a piece of chicken and dipped it in some ketchup. "Nothing really, but at least you would know. Kind of like why I wanted to know what it was like when you met the Rolling Stones."

"To be honest with you, after all those years, when I finally did find out about him, it didn't mean anything to me. He wasn't even a memory."

"Perhaps it was just for some peace of mind," I said. "Like me wanting to know why you ran away from us."

My father nodded. "I know I should have done more for you and Danny, and that has been something that I have had to live with and try to make up for," he said. "I am sorry that I couldn't have done more. I know I should have."

It was the first time my dad had ever said he was sorry.

It was getting late, and my father still had an hour-long drive home after he returned the truck to his friend.

"How long are you going to be in town?"

Someone opened the door and a blast of wind rushed in. My father and I turned to see the gray sky threatening rain. It's a good thing we finished when we did. Maybe if it got any colder, it would snow.

"Until the day after tomorrow," I said, swirling a soggy, cold fry in a pool of ketchup. "That's when I fly back to Portland."

"You wouldn't want to come over for dinner," my dad said, putting his hand on my shoulder.

"*And after that struggle, Brad finally reeled in that northern,*" the narrator from the fishing program said. "*That's one mighty fine pike.*"

My dad and I looked at the TV and grinned.

On the fishing program, the camera panned to the right, showing Brad holding up the fish. Standing next to Brad was his father, gleaming for the camera.

"*Now that's one very proud father and his son,*" the narrator added.

"Why not," I said.

Wind Chill Factor

We buried Paul today.

He picked a lousy time to take his life—the middle of winter with the temperature and wind-chill factor right around fifty or sixty below. It was so cold at St. Hyacinth's Cemetery that only the pallbearers, immediate family, and a few friends braved the cold, wind and steadily falling temperatures for the graveside services. Everyone else stayed in their cars, motors running, heaters blasting.

I swore that when Paul's wife wept over the silver casket, her tears turned to ice as soon as they hit the cold surface. In a black Lincoln, the other pallbearers and I stamped our feet and blew on our hands. It didn't do any good, but it gave us something to do before we headed back to town. I've never felt cold like I did that day. Sure, there was that time I went ice fishing with my old man and we sat in a freezing ice shanty on the slough south of town and I cried until he had enough and we hiked back to the car. I thought that was cold until the day of Paul's funeral.

Paul would have never taken his life in the summer. He would have been too busy playing softball for Flo's Tap in the tavern league, water skiing on the Illinois River, or fishing along the shores of Lake Senachawine. And he would have never sat in the car in his garage with the motor running in spring because he would have been out working in his parents' garden every chance he got. And fall? Forget it. If he wasn't spending his weekends watching college and NFL football, he was heading off to places like Galena and St. Charles for antiquing.

At least he waited until after the holidays. With Paul, timing was everything. Something he picked up as the lead guitarist of our band, Shippingsport Blues. In all the years I knew him, he never was late for anything. Except he had to pick the worst cold snap in one hundred years to die.

His wife called with the news. I calmed her down as best I could. She wasn't the one who discovered his body. She was spared that terrible fate; when Paul didn't come home, she called her father. The first place he looked was in the garage. Found him inside the car. His family requested that I be one of his pallbearers along with the other guys who had been in our band. He was *your* friend, Paul's widow reminded me. The phone dropped out of my hands. Yeah, I told her when I finally regained my composure.

That was one word I could never wrap my mind around: *pallbearer*. The origin of the word is from a pall—a heavy white cloth—which is linked symbolically to the white garments worn at a baptism. The introductory rites of a funeral ceremony are done so to signify the death and rebirth of a person during a baptism, symbolically linking these two events in a person's life. In some funeral ceremonies, the pall is draped over the coffin, as one final, symbolic link. Put it all together and the term *pallbearer* is used to signify someone who bears the coffin that the pall covers.

There was another meaning to the word—to cast a pall over something—which pretty much summed up my mood when I agreed to carry Paul to his final resting place.

The last time I talked to him was a week ago when he'd found me at Vinnie's, a decrepit hole-in-the-wall haunt on the east end of town where I sometimes ended up when I wanted to be alone. I thought for sure he had found out and was going to cold-cock me; instead, he just wanted to talk. He talked about how he was going to go back to school and how happy he was with Missy. And I believed him. After all, he was *still* my friend.

"You are one lucky dude," I had said, choosing my words carefully. "You got it all."

Three days later, he was dead.

At the funeral home last night, everyone had talked about how great Paul was in hushed voices. He wasn't that great of a guy. He had his faults just like the rest of us. Friends who hadn't seen him in years, even though we all lived in the same town, talked about how much they were going to miss him. When he was alive, these same people didn't have the time of the day for him. But there they were, swapping memories, punching in digits on their phones, and promising they would stay in touch.

Not everyone was so kind. Someone mentioned how his wife was stepping out on him again; said how he had bumped into Paul at JoJo's the night he died.

"He looked awful," the person said. "Said he had a fight with Missy about something and went out for a drink. It was so awful cold that night. I probably should have given him a ride."

"His father-in-law found him slumped over in the front seat with the motor running, the garage door closed, and the windows rolled up," another hushed voice said.

"Coldest winter in fifty years," another person said. "If you're out in that kind of weather for any length of time, there's not much hope."

"I don't understand," one of Paul's friends from high school said. "He had a lovely, caring wife, a good job, and a good home. Did you know his wife was a former Mendota Sweet Corn Festival queen?"

In the other room, Missy sat by herself on one side of the room; Paul's family sat on the other side.

"I never knew what Paul saw in her," another hushed voice said.

That was enough for me. I left the room in search of a drink.

I hurried out into the freezing night and quickly slipped into a bar just down the street for a shot and a beer. I was no better than the people I listened to talk about my friend. Paul and I had had a falling out a while back. I accused him of sleeping with my girlfriend while I was away at college. Of course, he denied it, but I had a hunch he was lying. We ended up not talking to each other for almost a year.

We all have our own crosses to bear; at the moment, mine was heavier than others.

After the graveside services, most of the mourners went to a reception at his house, but I didn't want to go. It would have been too awkward. Instead, I met up with a few friends whom I hadn't seen in ages for dinner at the Uptown, this swank eatery on First Street. A few continued those hushed conversations we'd had at the funeral home the night before. Some even cracked a few jokes about some stuff Paul did, like the time we all did acid and sat on the dry bridge east of town and waved to people going to work. When I was in college, one of my favorite films was *The Big Chill*, which was about a group of friends who get together after the funeral of their friend. Paul and I loved that movie. He would have approved of tonight, though if he were here, he would have been pissed that grilled swordfish was no longer on the menu.

Then someone had to bring up his wife again. This person knew she slept around; she'd heard it from Missy's hairdresser. Paul knew, too, when he proposed to her. He had hoped that once she met the right person, she would quit her running around and settle down. Boy, was he *ever* wrong about that. I motioned for another drink and was glad when someone started talking about something else besides Paul and the weather.

After everyone had gone home, promising to stay in touch for the umpteenth time, I drove down First Street to Volk's Tap. Famous for its pork tenderloin sandwiches, it was one of my favorite watering holes. It was also the only place open. There were only two other patrons inside, and they sat at the far end of the bar watching a rerun of *M*A*S*H*. Outside the wind howled. Forecasters predicted the temperature would drop even further and that coupled with the wind chill factor, it would be seventy below. A cold-weather advisory had been issued; the state police advised motorists to stay home.

I ordered a shot of Jack Daniels and stared at my reflection in the mirror behind the bar. I looked like shit but felt even worse. I quickly drank the shot and felt the whiskey coursing through my body, but I just couldn't seem to warm up. Maybe if I finally drank enough on this three-day drunk of mine, it would eventually numb me. I motioned for another. Damn, it was cold. Coldest day in my life. Ever.

Night Shift

Clayton Bennett was looking forward to a quiet evening at work until he heard someone banging on the door to the supply office; the next thing he knew, his buddy Doug Lawson fell into the room.

Someone had done a number on Doug's face. It looked as if he had gone a couple of rounds with Roberto Duran. He had one black eye—with the other one swollen and partially open—a fat bloodied lip, and cuts across his chin and forehead. Clayton looked down at Doug's bloodied knuckles. He must have got in a few punches or deflected the ones that pummeled his face. He also reeked of rum and Seco Herrerano, a local firewater that was usually mixed with milk.

"Where can I get a piece?" Doug said, staggering to a cot on the far side of the room and plopping down on it. The cot was used by Clayton and the other airmen who worked the night shift in the After Hours Support Unit, which began at four in the afternoon and ended at eight in the morning; when things were quiet, the airmen could sack out for a couple of hours.

Doug's request for a "piece" caught Clayton off guard but not totally. His friend's propensity for being a sloppy drunk was matched only by his propensity for histrionics. Knowing Doug, he probably got in the face or the faces of the wrong people. As for the why, Clayton suspected it involved a woman.

"What the hell happened?" Clayton rolled up his chair to the cot.

"I need a piece," Doug said again, spitting out blood. "Can you help me or not?"

"Why don't I help you get cleaned up and take you back to your room?" Clayton asked, quickly changing the subject. "You'll feel better in the morning."

"Don't patronize me," Doug said, lying down and stretching out on the cot.

"Maybe I should take you to the clinic and have someone take a look at you," Clayton suggested. "You look awful."

"Are you trying to be funny?"

"No, I'm just saying that I think someone should take a look at you."

"I'm fine," Doug said.

The telephone rang. It was the radar shack across the runway. A fuse had blown out in one of their scopes and it couldn't wait until morning. After Clayton had checked the daily supply printout book to make sure they had the fuse on hand and its location in the warehouse, he typed out an invoice.

"You wait here until I get back," Clayton said. "I won't be too long. Then we'll see about that piece."

Clayton didn't know what else to say, but at least it would keep Doug in his office until he got back. Then he'd figure out what to do. The warehouse was just down the street. The fuse would be easy to find; Clayton just wasn't too crazy about having to drive out to the radar shack in the middle of the night. Just last week, one of the guys working out there spotted a panther. He was also wasn't too crazy about leaving Doug alone in the office.

Doug licked his bloodied lip, put his hands behind his head, and closed his eyes. "Do what you've gotta do."

Clayton grabbed his Motorola radio in case anyone else called while he was out of the office. When he checked on Doug one more time before he left, his friend had already passed out.

Clayton first met Doug not long after he arrived at Howard Air Force Base on the Pacific side of the Panama Canal Zone in early 1977. He heard him yelling on the phone in the hallway of their barracks late one night. The air conditioning had been broken for a week and in the stifling, muggy Panama weather, it made sleeping impossible. Doug had somehow gotten the phone number of the wing commander, a full-bird colonel, and complained to the colonel's aide about the broken air conditioning, demanding that something be done about it or else. Clayton thought for sure Doug would be slapped with an Article 15, which was the military's nonjudicial punishment for the way he talked to the aide. But it turned out that the aide had been in the

101st Airborne in Vietnam—the same division Doug had been in—and was quite sympathetic to Doug's ranting. Two days later, the air conditioning was fixed.

The next time Clayton ran into his friend was on the flight line. Doug worked in Transient Alert, which was the Air Force equivalent of a gas station attendant. They were the guys who drove the "follow me" trucks, parked the aircraft, checked the oil, cleaned the bugs of the windshield—those sorts of things. On this particular night, it was a C-47 from the Chilean Air Force that needed a couple cans of oil.

Clayton pulled up to the aircraft and hopped out of his truck. He looked for Doug but couldn't find him anywhere.

"I'm up here!" a voice said from inside the aircraft.

Clayton looked up and saw his friend standing in the rear cargo door. Behind his friend, Clayton could see washing machines, television sets, tires, and other assorted household goods crammed into the plane.

"What the—" Clayton began.

Doug walked down the portable gangway that was mounted on the back of a truck, carrying some bottles of Chilean wine.

"They go shopping in Miami once a month for their commander," Doug said, holding up the bottles of wine. "Which do you prefer, red or white?"

Over the next couple of months, Clayton and Doug worked the same after hours shifts and got to know each other well; Clayton learned that Doug had been in 'Nam and drove a taxi in D.C. for a few months after the war, before he decided to re-enlist in the Air Force. Doug also had a reputation for drinking a lot and not holding his alcohol very well. More often than not, this didn't bode well for him with the scrapes he got into with some guys in the barracks, not to mention other military personnel at other bases in the Canal Zone. One weekend he pissed off a group of sailors from Rodman; the next weekend, it was a trio of paratroopers from Kobbe, an Army base adjacent to the air base. In both instances, Clayton and some buddies from the barracks had to step in and prevent Doug from having the shit kicked out of him.

This night, Doug must have gone solo.

On their days off, Clayton and Doug explored the Canal Zone—even taking the train across the Isthmus a few times—and at night, they'd prowl the steamy underside of Panama City in its bars and clubs, carousing with the Colombian hostesses and drinking as much rum as their bodies would withstand.

One of those nights, at the Ovalo Inn, as they imbibed a steady flow of Cuba Libres, which had the same effect on their souls as a truth serum, Doug opened up about 'Nam and the time he shot a teenage VC girl when she pulled an AK-47 on him.

Although he was pretty numb from all the rum he had drunk, he had still shuddered when he told the story. "I just wanted you to know." He never mentioned it again and Clayton never asked him. It was his ghost and he would deal with it the best way he could.

This night revealed a side of his friend that Clayton had never seen before. Clayton had only seen him mad one other time—the time he got really upset with him when Clayton messed around with the equalizer on Doug's new stereo system.

"Don't ever touch my shit again," Doug had said with a hooded stare, "or I'll kill you."

Clayton never knew whether he was joking or meant it.

From the supply squadron, which was located on the second floor of the transient barracks on base, to the warehouse, was less than a five-minute drive. It took Clayton another ten minutes to find the fuse, and then another five minutes to drive to the radar shack, a small trailer crammed with radios, monitors, and scopes. Clayton knew the two airmen who worked the night shift repairing and calibrating the equipment. When they got bored and wanted someone to play cards with them, they usually ordered some low-priority items. When Clayton walked in, the two airmen, Roy Gordon and Vince Toliver, were playing cards. Roy looked a bit like Potsie from *Happy Days* and took a lot of ribbing from the guys in his squadron.

"What took you so long?" Roy asked, looking up from his cards. "What's the matter, you get lost?"

"Ante up, Potsie," Vince said, sipping on a Dr. Pepper. "Are you going to play cards or what?"

"How many times have I told you not to call me that?" Roy said, throwing down two damp dollar bills. "I see your dollar and raise you another buck."

Clayton laughed, holding up the fuse and the invoice. "Who wants to sign for this?"

"Come on and play a couple hands with us," Roy said, taking the fuse and signing the invoice.

"Yeah, the way old Potsie's playing tonight, you might get lucky," Vince said, laughing.

"Knock it off," Roy said.

"I really ought to get back," Clayton said.

"Come on, don't be a lightweight," Roy persisted. "Just a few hands."

Clayton looked at his watch. He had only been gone for twenty minutes. Another fifteen or twenty minutes wouldn't hurt. Besides, Doug was probably still passed out on the cot. He was in no shape to go wandering off somewhere and in no shape to exact whatever revenge he wanted on the person or people who messed him up. At least, that's what Clayton hoped. To be honest, Clayton was fed up with Doug's antics. Maybe if Clayton were lucky, Doug wouldn't be there when he got back.

"Sure," Clayton said. "Deal me in."

Clayton pulled up a chair and tore off a Dr. Pepper from the plastic six-pack ring. He shoved a handful of popcorn in his mouth and waited for Vince to deal. Five hands later, he was up five bucks.

"Hey, did you hear what happened to one of your buddies from the barracks?" Roy asked.

"Who?" Clayton inquired.

"Lawson," Roy said. "You know, the guy who works in transient alert. I heard he got into some fight or something. Some grunts jumped him walking out of Kobbe earlier this evening."

Clayton's eyes widened.

"Fucking grunts," Vince muttered.

"Cash me in, boys," Clayton said, worried that he might have stayed too long. "I'd better get back to the office."

On his way back to the supply squadron, Clayton felt bad for not having gone back to his office as quickly as he'd said he would. Doug looked pretty awful. Maybe he should have insisted on taking him to the clinic. He might have suffered a concussion or something.

When he walked into his office ten minutes later, Doug was gone.

Worried about his friend, Clayton checked to see whether Doug had gone back to their barracks across the street from the supply building.

Doug's roommate, Hector, came to the door with a towel wrapped around him. Inside, Clayton could see a young Panamanian woman with her hands clasped over her bare breasts.

"This better be good, Bennett," Hector said. "As you can see, I'm a little busy."

"I'm looking for Doug," Clayton said, out of breath. "He came to my office all bloody and beaten up."

"Haven't seen him all night," Hector said, not too concerned about the welfare of his roommate. "Have you checked the day room?"

Clayton checked the day room and the latrines on the third and fourth floors, but there was no sign of his friend.

On his way of out of the barracks, he bumped into his buddy Ted Campbell, better known as Moose, who had his arm around a woman he most likely picked up at the NCO Club.

"Hey, Moose," Clayton said. "You haven't seen Lawson, have you?"

Moose nodded. "I saw him earlier in the evening. He said he was going to the carnival on Kobbe. He was pretty messed up."

Every year, Howard and Kobbe took turns holding a festival and carnival for service members and their families. This year, it was held on Kobbe. While it was mainly family-oriented, the beer tent was a big hit with the single enlisted. Cheap beer and eighteen-year-olds brimming with testosterone were not a healthy combination. That's probably where Doug messed with the wrong soldiers.

"Listen, you wouldn't happen to have any weed, would you?" Moose gestured with his thumb and forefinger as he pretended to toke an imaginary marijuana joint.

Clayton shook his head. "Thanks, Moose."

After he had left the barracks, Clayton drove around the base hoping to find his friend. Most places, such as the BX shoppette, snack bar, and NCO Club were already closed, but on the off chance that Doug might have wandered back to them, he drove past each one. He was worried about deep, concrete drainage ditches that crisscrossed the base. A person in Doug's mental and drunken state could easily fall in one of them and end up with a couple of broken bones—if the snakes didn't get to you first.

Clayton also went to the base clinic, but there was no sign of Doug there. On his way back to the office, Clayton drove past the Security Police Squadron and thought about stopping, but what would he tell them? He was worried that his friend was going to do something crazy. They would have his ass in the sling for not reporting it earlier. Shit like that could get a guy redlined for promotion, busted, or maybe even get booted out of the Air Force with a less-than-honorable discharge.

Where the hell did he go?

He remembered another time his friend ended up on the wrong end of a fist to his face. It was at the NCO club on one of the nights the club had an outdoor barbecue. Club members sat at tables set up in the parking lot, burgers and steaks sizzled on grills made from fifty-five-gallon drums, and a Filipino band, The Kiwis, played on a flatbed trailer. Clayton and Doug were there with some buddies from the barracks. Seated next to them were some Marines and their girlfriends.

40

Doug said hello to one of the ladies, mistaking her for a girl from the Ancon Inn, one of the bars downtown. That was his first mistake. His second mistake was spilling a drink on her boyfriend as he staggered past the table. The Marine stood up and pushed Doug away. Finally, Doug's third mistake was taking a sloppy swing at the Marine, who responded with a hard uppercut to Doug's nose. Blood streamed everywhere as Doug staggered back. Before Clayton and the others could intervene, Doug grabbed a chair and smacked the Marine on the side of his head. The ensuing fight had to be broken up by security police.

Clayton remembered that Doug had enjoyed every moment of it, even though he got the shit kicked out of him. He wasn't worried about what the police or his first sergeant would do. Clayton and the rest of their buddies from the barracks were pissed at Doug after they were banned from the club for a month for the fracas.

When Clayton pulled into the parking lot next to the supply building, he spotted Doug walking into the chow hall across the street. After he had parked his truck, dashed across the street, and ran up the flight of stairs into the chow hall, Clayton found his friend slumped in a chair in the back with two trays of food in front of him. It didn't look like Doug was too enthused about the food he had selected; he eyed a Spanish omelet with contempt as Clayton pulled up a chair and sat down across from him.

"Jesus, Doug," Clayton said with a sigh of relief. "I've been looking for you everywhere."

"And you found me," Doug said, swirling a strip of bacon in a pool of ketchup.

"Are you okay?" Clayton asked. "You really gave me a scare earlier."

"It's okay, Bennett," Doug said, twisting his puffy lips into a smile and winking at him with his one good eye. "Don't be such a pussy."

Clayton beetled his eyebrows. "Pussy? What the hell, Doug? I thought for sure you were going to kill the guy who beat you up."

"Jesus, Bennett," Doug said, with a twinkle in his good eye. "Whatever gave you *that* idea?"

"You wanted a piece for chrissakes."

Doug laughed with a rich, throaty chuckle as he pushed the other tray of food across the table to his friend. "Eat up, Bennett. You look a little peaked."

Clayton gazed at the Spanish omelet and attacked it with relish. For better or worse, he never could stay angry at his friend for too long.

Killing Geckos

Kun-hee woke up screaming; a jingjok—a tiny, cute reptilian creature, part of the gecko family—had fallen from the ceiling and landed on her face.

"Get it off me!" she screamed. "Kill it!"

"We're not supposed to kill them," I said, trying to calm her down as best I could. "It's unlucky. I read it in my guidebook."

"I don't care. Kill it!" she screamed again, running into the bathroom.

It was our first *real* trip together, but she complained about one thing after another. Thailand *wasn't* everything her Korean guidebook said it was. If it wasn't the food or accommodations, it was the weather or Third World squalor. About the only thing, we agreed on, after we'd had our fill of golden Buddhas and temples in Bangkok, were a couple of days on Koh Samui, but that quickly turned out to be just as bad as everything else.

The resort was nothing like the pictures we'd seen in a brochure three days earlier. The hotel was far from the main beaches—it had little beach to speak of, just a strip of rocky sand—the bungalows were not air conditioned, there was no hot water, and now, to Kun-hee's dismay, they were crawling with jingjok.

"Did you get it?" she asked, poking her head out of the bathroom.

"I think so," I lied, holding up one of my sandals as proof of my murder weapon.

"Are you sure?"

"No."

She gave me her best, "I'm not through with you" look, got into bed, and rolled on her side. I followed her into bed and draped my arm around her. One faked jingjok death ought to have been good enough for make-up sex, but Kun-hee had already figured that out.

"I can't believe you didn't kill it." She lifted my arm from her chest and pushed it away. "Not now. I'm tired."

I turned over and watched another jingjok climb the wall. Just three more days and we'd leave this paradise hell and be back to Seoul's noise and chaos. I didn't know which was worse, here or there, as I gave the jingjok a wink and hoped it had more friends.

Yuki no Sasayaki

("Whispers in the Snow")

Her name was Yukiko. I knew she would break my heart the first time I laid eyes on her that cold, slate-gray day in Kofu as she walked into school, her long straight black hair flowing behind her.

Although I saw her around the school, we hadn't been properly introduced. It wasn't until she came to my apartment on the day she moved in with a small gift—customary in Japan when a person moved into an apartment to give gifts to the other tenants—that we finally had the chance to talk.

All I knew about her was that she was in her late fifties, but she looked much younger. Supposedly, she was divorced. She lived alone at the far end of our two-story complex across the street from a small lake and bamboo grove. She taught children's classes—classes that needed a bilingual teacher—as well as Japanese classes to foreigners living in Kofu. Before she came to our school, she had taught English at a school in Niigata.

When I learned she was from Niigata, I told her how much I loved Kawabata's *Snow Country*. The next day, there was a copy of the book in my mailbox with a note attached: *Dear Jonathan Sensei, Thank you for your kindness and friendship*. I don't know how she got an English translation of the book so fast.

More gifts followed. Sometimes she made me an *O-bento*—a Japanese-style boxed lunch that consisted of rice, meat or fish, and vegetables. Other times she dropped off bread, fruit, even beer.

"You'd better watch out," Peter, a teacher from Canada, snickered one day when I told him about the gifts. "She's probably got an angle or something."

"She's just a very lovely woman," I said. "She's just trying to be friendly."

"Well, you know what they say about women over the age of twenty-five in Japan, don't you?" he said with a sarcastic tone.

"No, I don't."

"They're like a Christmas cake," he said. "No good after the twenty-fifth."

In Japan, many Japanese celebrated Christmas with colorful and decorative Christmas cakes.

"Excuse me?" I said.

"Women older than twenty-five have a difficult time finding a husband. That's probably why she's been so nice to you."

I glared at Peter. He could be such a jerk at times. "No, she's just a nice woman."

"Ha!" Peter said. "You'll see."

In school, Yukiko and I sometimes ate lunch together in the lunchroom. She helped me with my Kanji—the Chinese pictograms used in modern Japanese. She would gently hold my fingers and guide them as I made each stroke. She wore a faint, musky perfume that smelled of sandalwood with a hint of vanilla. One day she noticed that I wore wooden Buddhist prayer beads on my wrist.

"Are you Buddhist?" she asked, pointing to the wooden prayer beads, *ozuju*, which I wore as a bracelet.

I nodded.

"Have you ever been to Kuonji Temple?" she asked.

I had heard about the temple from one of the teachers at school. It was most famous for its 287 "steps of enlightenment" that led up the side of the mountain to the main temple complex.

"Not yet," I said.

"You should go someday."

I was surprised when she showed up in my academic writing class the following week. She sat in the front and wrote down everything that I said. Whenever I looked at her, she blushed and averted her eyes to the amusement of another middle-aged woman in the class. For homework, I told the students they had to write two paragraphs in their journals about an emotional experience and its effect on their lives. I called the assignment a "scar story."

The following class, after I collected their homework assignments, I sat at the kitchen table in my tiny two-room apartment and read and graded their journals. Most of the "scar stories" were about minor childhood accidents, like the one from Kenzo—who wrote about the scar on his forehead, which was the result of falling off a swing when he was three years old—or the one from Mika, who had one on her palm from the time she cut her hand while peeling an apple. For the most part, the scar stories were harmless and innocuous until I came to Yukiko's.

A week after my baby died, I went down to the lake near our apartment. I wanted to kill myself for having lost my child; instead, I sat underneath a maple tree and squeezed the milk out from my breasts that had been for my baby. I dug my fingernails into my breasts hard enough to draw blood. Together, blood and milk mixed. Every day for a month, I would do the same thing. At night, I would cry myself to sleep. My doctor told me that I might not be able to have a child again. My husband and I hardly talked during this time....

"I'm so sorry, Yukiko," I said, handing back her journal the next time we had class. She had waited until everyone else had left. I still felt a little uncomfortable for having read something so personal and tragic.

"My husband and I divorced shortly after that," she said, with tears in her eyes. "He moved back to Tokyo, and I never saw him again. He married another woman a few years later. They had two children."

After that class, I didn't see her at school the next day or the day after. Maybe she had been embarrassed by writing about her life, opening up to me the way that she did. I didn't see her around the apartment complex, either. The following Monday, when I had my Japanese class with her, she didn't show up.

When I inquired at the office whether Yukiko was sick or something, Keiko, the school's administrative assistant, only said that there had been some family emergency, and she'd had to go home.

She wasn't at school the following week, either. The school canceled her Japanese classes for the rest of the month. Two weeks later, there was a knock on my door. It was Yukiko.

"My ex-husband died," she said slowly. "I went to pay my respects to his family. They were good to me."

I made us some green tea, and together we sat on the hardwood floor on cushions with our legs underneath the *kotatsu*—a small table with a heating lamp. When our feet touched, at first, I pulled mine back, but our legs touched again. When she brought the cup to her small pink lips, letting the steam drift in front of her round face, it was the first time I had looked deep into her dark, almond-shaped eyes. I felt as though I could look straight into her soul, and the more I gazed at them, the more they pulled me in.

"I missed you," she said as she lowered the cup. "I'm sorry I didn't tell you before I left. It was all so sudden."

I nodded. "That's okay, I understand. I missed you, too."

She looked at me and smiled. "I just told Keiko that I would be gone for a few weeks on a family matter."

"I know. She told me it was about your family."

Yukiko nodded. I could already see her eyes filling with tears. She set the cup down and took out a lace handkerchief from a pocket of her jacket. She dabbed her eyes.

"Then you understand what I must do."

I nodded.

Before she left, she made good on her promise to take me to Kuonji Temple. It started snowing when we left Kofu and by the time we got to the base of the mountain, where the temple sat, the snow had begun to come down heavy. We exited the taxi we had taken from the train station and started up the snow-covered steps.

Halfway toward the top, Yukiko slipped on the snowy surface, but I caught her before she fell. She looked into my eyes and smiled as we stood in a snowy embrace. Once we made it to the top, we discovered we were the only ones in the temple. We took off our boots and padded across the cold wooden floor. We lit incense and sat on brown cushions in front of the Buddha statuary. Yukiko softly chanted some scripture as she fingered the wooden beads on the rosary around her wrist.

Later, when we left and slowly moved across the temple compound, Yukiko let me hold her hand. We did not speak. There was nothing left for us to say. The only sounds were our breathing and the sound each snowflake made when it landed.

For Emily

Emily finally got around to boxing up her late husband's clothes to donate to Goodwill. For months, she painstakingly hung on to them as though this simple act would guarantee her that the memories she had of him would never be lost. She slowly worked her way down the strata of shirts, sweaters, and trousers entombed in a steamer trunk in the attic. Even though it had been months and years since his clothes had been relegated to the attic, she went through the pockets methodically out of habit, instead of searching for some long lost memory of their time together.

At the bottom of the trunk, she removed the last of her husband's clothes, a brown tweed jacket with the leather patches on the elbows. She still remembered when she'd bought the jacket. He had just started teaching at a downstate university, so she had bought it for him at Paul Koehler's, a men's shop in downtown Bloomington. He had looked so handsome and dashing in it. He had reminded her of Steve McQueen and a jacket he wore in *Bullitt*. She lifted the jacket out of the trunk and held it in front of her. Although the jacket still carried a distinct hint of mothballs, if she closed her eyes and imagined hard enough, she could smell his favorite brand of pipe tobacco.

Emily was so caught up with inventorying her husband's clothing that she didn't see her oldest daughter, Alicia, standing at the far end of the attic. After months of going around and around with her three kids about whether she could take care of the house on her own, Emily had finally given in and decided to sell the house and move into a condominium on the outskirts of town. It was for the best, they told her though Emily thought otherwise.

"Mom, do you have anything more to go to Goodwill?" Alicia asked, brushing a wisp of brown hair that had fallen down across her sweaty, dirty forehead.

"Just a sec," her mother said, as she held up the jacket.

"That was Dad's favorite jacket, wasn't it?" Alicia asked, pulling up a chair and sitting down across from her mother.

Her mother nodded. "He loved this jacket."

Alicia smiled. "I remember the photograph you had of him wearing it when he won the Teacher of the Year award."

"Oh, that's right," her mother said. "You know, I always thought that if your father weren't a teacher, he would have made a fine actor. Did you know that he once auditioned for a role in a movie that was filmed in Pontiac?"

"Yes, you told me that story many times."

"It wasn't a big part or anything, but he was called back twice. Who knows what would have happened had he gotten that role," Emily said as she started to go through the pockets of the jacket. "Nonetheless, he acted in community theater for many years. He once played Harold Hill in *The Music Man*."

"I remember when you dragged us kids to see him," Alicia said. "He was a good singer."

Emily smiled and reached into the inside pocket. Her fingers touched something that felt like cardboard, and she pulled out two concert ticket stubs.

"What are those, Mom?"

"Concert ticket stubs." She heaved a sigh and stared at the tickets. Of all the things he could have thrown away, he had to keep these.

"Can I see?"

Emily fingered the tickets and felt a sadness rising inside of her as she passed them to her daughter.

"Simon and Garfunkel?" Alicia asked as she looked at the ticket stubs. "Who were they?"

"They were very popular in the '60s. Your father loved them," Emily explained. "He said they were America's poet laureates along with Bob Dylan during the 1960s. He taught some of their song lyrics in one of his literature classes. They had a brief comeback in the early '80s."

Alicia handed the ticket stubs back to her mother. Emily looked at the date on the tickets. It was funny how her husband had forgotten all about them in the jacket and how she had missed them before. One thing was for certain: thirty-five years later, the scars still ran deep.

"Mom, is there something wrong?" Alicia asked.

"What was that, dear?"

"Are you okay? You look as though you've seen a ghost."

That ghost was alive and well and living on the other side of town. Emily still saw Mary Jo from time to time at the supermarket or the beauty salon where she had her hair done once a month. Ben had said their relationship was purely a professional one when Emily found out, but in the back of her mind, Emily had always had her doubts even though she had forgiven him. Ben had told her that he was helping her with her thesis which explained all the late-night meetings and dinners—though their drinks at the Lamplighter Inn had fueled her suspicions. There were some things a person could keep secret in a small town; there were others that one couldn't.

Although Emily had debated confronting Mary Jo about the ticket stubs, there was no way she was going to be able to rest easy until she had. She had to know even if it broke her heart again.

When she pulled into the driveway, she saw a man on a riding lawnmower cutting grass in the front yard. The man shaded his eyes with his hand to see who it was as he steered the lawn mower back toward the house, but Emily had already hurried up the sidewalk to the front door.

"I was very sorry to hear about Ben's passing," Mary Jo said later in the kitchen, pouring Emily a cup of coffee. "I'm sorry we missed the funeral. We were vacationing in the Dells."

"I understand," Emily said. "It was all so sudden."

Mary Jo nodded, pouring herself a cup of coffee.

"The strangest thing happened the other day," Emily began. "I was going through Ben's clothes, and I came across some old concert ticket stubs."

"Really?" Mary Jo said, crinkling her nose. "You know there are folks on eBay who will pay good money for that kind of nostalgia. What concert was it?"

"Simon and Garfunkel."

Mary Jo's hand trembled as she set her cup down, trying not to telegraph too much of her surprise. "Oh really?"

"You wouldn't happen to know anything about that, would you?"

"Why do you ask?"

"Please, Mary Jo," Emily said, working up her courage. "You know what I mean."

"Is that what this visit is all about?" Mary Jo said, knocking over her cup of coffee. The coffee puddle seeped into the cotton red-and-white checked tablecloth. "I should have known better."

"Well, did YOU?" Emily asked, raising her voice.

Mary Jo smirked and regained her composure. "If it's any consolation, I really didn't care much for the concert. I was never into that kind of music. I would rather it have been the Stones or Led Zeppelin."

The back door opened and slammed shut. Emily glared at Mary Jo. It wasn't any consolation. It would never be any consolation as Benjamin Jr., now in his mid-thirties, but forever the spitting image of his father, shuffled into the kitchen.

"Who's this woman, Mother?" Benjamin asked, staring at Emily.

Black Roses

Glen sat in the corner booth of the Hollywood Diner and stared out one of the windows that separated the gray and red walls. He was delighted with the cool autumn day. It was one of those dark and gray days he loved being in the city despite the light drizzle that had been falling most of the morning. He held a cup of coffee to his lips and took pleasure in the richness and the warmth. On the cigarette-burned, graffiti-scarred table next to a half-eaten pastrami on rye, his drawing pad was open and waiting.

He normally waited until the lunch crowd had thinned out before he walked across the street from the bookstore he worked at on North Milwaukee Avenue. Although the bookstore gig helped pay the rent and put food on the table, he often plied his better-suited talents as a street artist in Wicker Park. When he wasn't joining other artists doing graffiti on the sides of buildings and other structures, he could be found at various locations around the neighborhood doing caricatures for the tourists who came to Wicker Park looking for something chic and upscale. Glen remembered a time when it was still cool to tell people you were from Wicker Park before the upscale bars and boutiques sprang up everywhere and chased away the coolness.

On this day, though, he hadn't gone to work. For the past two days, he had been installing an exhibition of street art at a friend's gallery. It was the first time that a section of actual artwork on the side of a building slated for demolition would be removed and set up inside a gallery.

He thought about calling his fiancée, Lydia, and apologizing again for last night. They were supposed to meet her parents for dinner at Mona's, an Italian restaurant on North Milwaukee, but he had forgotten the time, and by the time he remembered and called, Lydia had already gone to dinner. When he got home later that evening, he did his best to smooth things over, but she already had other designs for how the rest of the night was going to go.

"I can't believe you forgot about dinner with my parents," she said, standing in the middle of the living room with her hands on her hips. She had already slipped into a pair of sweatpants and a DePaul sweatshirt. Cold cream was smeared on her cheeks and forehead. On the table was a wedge-shaped red and green box with *Mona's* stenciled in white. She might have been angry, but at least she'd brought some food home for him.

"I said I was sorry," Glen said, eyeing the Mona's box. Judging from the size of the box, it was their world-famous deep-dish pizza. "What more do you want from me?"

"You knew about this for over a month. Couldn't you meet your friends another time to do whatever you do that you think is so important?"

"It is important, and it's making a name for myself."

"Making a name for you? Spray painting graffiti is the stuff done by gangs and delinquents."

He could have told here right there and then, but he wanted to surprise her at the opening of the exhibition the following Saturday. "You wouldn't understand."

"How many years has it been now? Five?"

"It takes time."

"We had a deal you could do this until you graduated, then you would take my father's offer to work in his company."

Glen tossed his drawing pad on a wooden drafting table and fished for his prescription in his bag. When Lydia wasn't looking, he popped two yellow pills into his mouth and washed them down with a small bottle of mineral water. He didn't like that Lydia was now supporting him any more than she did, though neither would admit it.

"Maybe we should postpone the wedding—unless, of course, you've forgotten about it, too," Lydia said, storming off to their bedroom and slamming the door.

Glen had never cared much for the offer her father had extended him. It wasn't that he didn't want the job—the money was good and it would immediately upgrade his lifestyle—but he felt like he was being bought out. He couldn't see himself answering the phone and hovering in the shadow of the man who would be his father-in-law.

The next morning Lydia didn't speak to him before she left for work. He found one of his recent nude sketches of her ripped and the pieces scattered across the hardwood floor.

Across the street, he watched a man and a woman walk out of a boarded-up flower shop. The man wore a long overcoat and a hat pulled down over his face. The woman, also wearing an overcoat, with her gray hair pulled back into a ponytail, carried a tattered Marshall Field's shopping bag. She pushed the man along the sidewalk. The man lost his balance and nearly fell onto the street.

The man, after regaining his balance, turned around and yelled at the woman. He shook his fist at the woman and arched his head back. The veins on his neck tightened. Glen thought for sure the man was going to hit the woman; instead, he grabbed the woman's left arm and pulled her along the sidewalk.

Glen watched the couple move across the street to the bus stop in front of the café. He noticed that the man carried a dozen black roses wrapped in thin gray paper. He heard the muffled yelling of the man. The woman continued to look the other way. The man and the woman walked side by side when the bus arrived. A young woman in a red dress stepped between them. She knocked the roses out of the man's hand. The man stopped yelling. He looked at the woman in the red dress with a disoriented expression that was more painful than troubled. The older woman knelt down and picked up the roses before they boarded the bus.

Glen turned away from the window and rubbed his knuckles and the inside of his hand. He still hadn't told Lydia about what the doctor had told him. For weeks, he had been experiencing tender, swollen joints in his hands. At first, he thought it was simply an occupational hazard of being an artist, plus the cold, damp Chicago autumn, but then he went to the doctor and was told that he was suffering from rheumatoid arthritis. Although it hadn't advanced too far, the doctor warned Glen that it could get worse with time. The doctor put Glen on a regime of medication that included both steroids and anti-inflammatory drugs.

A waitress approached with a fresh pot of coffee. It wasn't the usual waitress, Madge, with her strawberry blonde hair piled high into a beehive, her body squeezed into a tight-fitting pink uniform that bulged in all the wrong places and crackled from all the starch she used when she ironed it, as she moved from one table to the next, referring to men as, *Hon* and *Darlin'* and to women, *Sugar*. The new waitress was young and inexperienced in the art of flirtatious banter for getting tips. Instead of asking Glen whether he wanted more coffee, she swooped in with the glass Bunn pot and filled his cup too quickly. Coffee slopped out of the cup and spilled on the table. She apologized and wiped the spill with her stained apron.

He turned back around and stared out the window.

Glen had one more cup of coffee and finished his sandwich before he left. He crossed the street and entered the boarded-up flower shop, but not before he saw the message of "Deliveries in the back" that someone had scrawled near the entrance in what looked like red lipstick. Inside, the shop smelled of burnt wood and smoke. The plants were bathed in a fluorescent pallor, which gave them a plastic, sickly appearance. He moved through the shop quickly, his eyes darting past the plants as he approached the sales counter in the back.

A young woman working in the back room walked out. She wore faded jeans and a T-shirt underneath a leather jacket. Her dark copper hair was cut short and spiked on top. Glen recognized her from one of the dance clubs he frequented. He may have even danced with her at one time, long ago in the past that no longer seemed like his anymore.

She pulled out a pen from a pocket on her jacket, grabbed an order pad, and leaned over the counter.

"Can I help you?" she asked.

Glen looked around. He spotted a cooler behind the counter. The cooler contained carnations and roses.

"A dozen black roses," he replied.

The woman looked up at Glen and sharply snapped the gum she was chewing. Glen noticed that her left hand was bandaged.

"That's a special order."

Glen looked at his watch.

"How long will it take?"

She snapped her gum again. "Give me an hour. I'm here by myself. I have a wedding and a funeral ahead of you."

Glen appreciated the irony as he turned and walked back outside. He stood in front of the flower shop and gazed at the El tracks in the distance. A train coming from downtown screeched and shuddered to a stop. A huddled mass of black and gray exited the train and moved amoebae-like across the platform and out of the station. He took out a pack of cigarettes from his pea coat and stuck one in one his mouth. The rain had stopped, but the sky was still overcast. The chill in the air was bearable.

Last night and this morning bothered him. It was a mistake. He and Lydia had a satisfying relationship. He was happy.

He had met Lydia the week he moved to the city. They had bumped into each other at a street fair in Wicker Park where he was making five bucks a pop, drawing caricatures. He drew one of Lydia. She liked it so much she asked him to draw another one. A week later they were dating. A month later he moved in with her.

Their relationship was fine for the first three months. He worked six days a week at the gallery and took a few classes toward his MFA at the Art Institute. Lydia completed her masters at DePaul, and landed a job with an advertising agency on Michigan Avenue. There was talk about a larger apartment, a trip to Europe, and marriage.

It was only after she told him that her father wanted Glen to come and work with him that he and Lydia had the first of many arguments that inevitably ended up being about money and Glen's future.

"You can't do this forever, can you Glen?" she asked him one afternoon after they had make-up sex after one of their arguments, one that she had lost, but only because she let him think that he had won.

He could have told her right then and there what the doctor had told him, but he didn't. Not being able to sketch or paint anymore was just as worse as losing Lydia.

He leaned up against the building and stared at the side of a brick building opposite a vacant lot and a boarded-up Mexican restaurant. Whereas most passers-by wouldn't give the nondescript building a second look, the barren wall was a canvas waiting for him to create. That was something Lydia could never understand. She thought of art in tangible, traditional forms and symmetry; he thought of it as wild, evocative and irregular. Her world was filled with Monet and Van Gogh; his was filled with Banksy and Fekner.

When he arrived back at their apartment an hour later, Lydia was already home. He heard water running in the bathroom. He made a pot of coffee and grabbed a croissant he had picked up on his way home. He sat down at the kitchen table and picked up the black roses. He carefully untied the red ribbon and removed the gray paper. Some of the black paint had smeared onto the paper, which resembled a Rorschach ink blot. He stared at it for a few seconds contemplating its insignificance before he crumpled up the paper and tossed it into a trashcan.

He found a red vase and filled it with water. He placed the roses in the vase one at a time. When he was finished, he set the vase in the middle of the table and lit a cigarette. He didn't notice Lydia's suitcase and overnight bag in the hallway.

He looked out the window. He noticed the woman from the flower shop standing outside the apartment, talking to a street vendor. She held a long-stemmed rose in her bandaged hand.

Lydia came out of the bathroom with a towel around her body and her hair wrapped in another one. She noticed the black roses immediately. She picked up one of the roses and smiled.

"I'm sorry about last night," he said.

Lydia nodded and twirled the rose between her fingers. "How was work today?"

"I didn't go into work. Derek asked me to come down to the gallery."

That was that. The cat was definitely out of the bag.

Lydia waited. She looked at the rose in her hand. There were two small dots of blood on her thumb. She threw the rose down.

"Why do you do this? You know the rent is due. You need to be a little more responsible."

"I know I should have told you, but—"

Lydia stood up and bumped the table. The vase fell over and shattered. The flowers slid across the film of water and fell to the floor. Water spilled onto his drawing pad. The water seeped through the drawing pad and smeared the two drawings.

Lydia moved back from the table.

"I'm sorry, Glen."

Glen shook her off. "I'll clean it up."

Lydia turned and walked out of the kitchen. Glen leaned back in the chair and lit another cigarette. He stared at the table. He picked up the portfolio and wiped off the water with his hand. When Lydia returned, she had gotten dressed and had her coat on. She carried the black and gray overnight bag over her shoulder. Her suitcase was in the other.

Glen's jaw dropped. It was worse than he'd thought.

"I've got to meet some clients in Atlanta. I'll be back the day after tomorrow," she said, moving from one screen to another on her BlackBerry. "Please think about my father's offer. It's for our future."

Glen should have been relieved, but he feared they were just delaying the inevitable, just like the medicine he took for his arthritis. He stared at the black roses in the plastic wastepaper basket. *Why did people say basket when in reality it was a plastic tub?*

Outside, on the street below, a horn sounded. Lydia dropped the BlackBerry into her purse and checked her lipstick in a mirror hanging on the wall.

"That's my taxi," Lydia kissed Glen on the cheek before she turned and left. Glen moved to a window and wiped off the beads of moisture that had formed on it. He looked down on the street below and waited for her to look up at him, but she only got into the taxi. He waited until the taxi drove off before he cleaned up the broken glass.

I should have told her.

The next morning Glen went back to the same café after he told the owner of the bookstore that he quit. Health reasons was what he told her. She looked up from her soy milk café latte and frowned. "I hope you get better," she said. She wrote him a check for half a month's work. There would be enough to pay the rent after all.

From memory, Glen sketched the man and the woman he saw arguing the previous day. *Funny, how emotions appear after the fact.* Glen added highlights to the man's exaggerated facial features. *Nothing is really premeditated. In the end, it's all cause and effect. There was no way of getting around that.* Moving to the city, the offer from Lydia's father, the arthritis crippling his hands—it was all right there in front of him. He couldn't stop what had already been put into motion.

When the waitress approached with a fresh pot of coffee, she sat down in the booth across from Glen.

"I'm really sorry about yesterday," she said.

Glen looked up and furrowed his brow. "Excuse me?"

"Yesterday, the coffee," she said, pointing to the coffee pot with a long finger. "I spilled it on your drawing pad."

"It was nothing," Glen said turning back to his drawing.

The waitress leaned over and examined what Glen had drawn. "You're good. Your lines are so angry and yet symmetrical. I like the contrast between the dark reflections of the sky with the empty, unshaded regions and the juxtaposition of the man and the woman. It's almost as though the empty spaces become the main point of emphasis."

Glen stopped and looked up at the waitress. That's when he noticed she had a tiny tattoo of a black rose behind her left ear.

Rain On Me

For the past eight years, I've been the drummer of the band Post Nasal Drip—until this morning, when Duane, the lead singer, called to tell me I had been replaced by a drum machine.

"Sorry, mate," Duane said, having recently acquired a British accent. "We had to make some changes."

"You can't fire me. I founded the band." I fumbled for my crumpled pack of smokes on the nightstand, and stuck a crooked Marlboro in my mouth.

"That's another thing. We're no longer Post Nasal Drip. We're now Kris Bermuda and the Triangles. That's Kris with a K."

"I take it you're Kris."

"With a *K*."

I rolled my eyes as I took a long drag off the cigarette and started coughing. I grabbed a glass of what I hoped was warm Coke and swigged enough to put out the fire in my throat.

"No hard feelings, right?"

"Fuck you, Duane."

"That's Kris. With a *K*."

"Fuck you, Kris with a *K*."

Click.

A cold shower and three cups of coffee later, I was ready to get to the bottom of my firing. There was no way in hell or Chicago that this was going to stand. Name change, drum machine or not, it was still my band.

Post Nasal Drip, or PND as our fans preferred to call us, rose from the ashes of the post-punk new wave apocalyptic musical wasteland, years before grunge became the wave and everyone wanted to be the next Nirvana, Pearl Jam, or Alice in Chains. Formed in Rockford back in the winter of 1979, we cut our teeth on the local bar/college circuit in Illinois, Iowa, and Wisconsin (trying *very* hard not to come across as another Cheap Trick wannabe) until we won a battle of the bands contest in Chicago (where we *actually* beat a Cheap Trick wannabe). Our synthesis of country, bluegrass, and blues, (we were huge CBGB fans after we took a road trip to the Big Apple to visit the holiest of the holy rock and roll shrines of our generation) was well received by fans and critics alike and thanks to a write-up in the Chicago Reader, we got a gig at Chicagofest on Navy Pier in the summer of 1981 and the kind of notoriety that bands would sell their souls to get.

That notoriety was the result of an appearance on *Good Morning Chicago* when Vince Vinyl our bassist and accordionist dropped the f-word during our interview with *GMC* host Suzy Vickson. Although none of our fans would have been up that early in the morning to catch the interview, the f-bomb and the debut of our new song, "Just a Dope from the 'Burbs," some mothers from M.A.L.L. (Mothers Against Lewd Lyrics) were definitely watching—and soon, to our best interests, we were on their radar screens. Once they started boycotting our shows, every punk within a 75-mile radius of the city started showing up at our concerts. We made the big time.

"Chet, what the fuck's going on?"

I had cornered Chet Wills, PND's lead guitarist, in the booth of the parking garage he worked at on North Wells, just down the street from the Up-Down Tobacco Shop. We were the two original members of PND, back when we were still calling ourselves Prairie Fire in high school before we decided on something more punk. Soft-spoken and laid-back, he was an excellent guitarist. He could hear a song one time and play it back note for note. Jazz, blues, country, rock, folk, bluegrass—nothing was out of his musical reach.

"Honestly, I had no idea what Kris had in mind when he asked me to go to Danny Balducci's Music World and buy a used Roland TR 808 drum machine," Chet said, taking some money from a driver leaving the garage. "He just handed me an envelope with money and told me to buy it. None of us knew that he was going to kick you out of the band."

I knew Chet wasn't in on it, but I just wanted to see what he knew or didn't know. I had never trusted Vince and as for the rhythm guitarist, Dirk McCready, he had only been with the band for a year and he certainly wasn't going to make any trouble. It was a coup, plain and simple. Chet sat down across from me on a stool and stuck a clove cigarette in his mouth. He offered me one, but I refused. I noticed that Chet had recently shaved his eyebrows, which now complemented his shaved head. He now looked like a cross between Lurch and Uncle Fester on *The Addams Family*.

"How could you let Duane do this to our band?"

"You know me, Tyler. I just show up and play what I'm asked to play. The money's still the same at the end of the night."

I thought about that scene in *The Blue Brothers* after Jake got out of prison and tried to put the band back together. Some of the band members formed a new band and were playing at a Holiday Inn. That's where I was seeing Chet in a few years.

"And what's with the shaved eyebrow look?" I asked.

"Come to the Metro tonight and you'll find out."

"Don't worry. I wouldn't want to miss it for the world."

The day went from bad to worse when I broke the news to my girlfriend, Cassandra, later that afternoon. Like me, Cassandra was a Chicago transplant. She had studied clothing and textile design at Southern Illinois University before she moved to the city to pursue her dreams. One night, she wandered into the club where we were playing and into my life. If there was anyone who could make sense out of what was happening, it was Cassandra.

She worked at a punk rock clothing store on Clark Avenue next to this club where we played a few times. When I walked in, she was sitting on a stool behind the cash register doing her nails. She had on a white T-shirt, black leather miniskirt with fishnet stockings, and her usual assortment of chains and spiked bracelets—standard issue for her job and lifestyle. She looked up as I walked in, blowing on her freshly painted nails.

"Babe, you'll never believe what happened this morning," I said, leaning across the counter and kissing her on her pale cheek, careful not to smudge the splotch of purple blush. She backed away as soon as she felt my lips touch her skin, as though I had leprosy.

"Rough day, huh?" she said with an air of disinterestedness as she inspected her nails for any flaws. "And that's why you didn't go into Tommy Jackson's again."

Tommy Jackson's was a music store in Evanston and my regular source of income on the two or three days a week I worked there convincing rich parents from the suburbs that buying a drum kit for their kids was in their best interests.

"Oh, shit. Today's Monday, isn't it?"

"I'm not calling and lying for you again."

"I got kicked out of the band."

Cassandra pulled the top off a tube of lipstick. "Is that so?"

"It was that weasel, Duane."

"This is probably not a good time, but you know things haven't been, you know, the way they used to be," she said, applying dark red lipstick.

"This is only a temporary setback," I said, having already thought about what I would tell Cassandra on my way to the shop. With Cassandra, I had to choose my words carefully. She read a lot of existential literature and was always trying to out-Camus me. "I've been looking for a reason to get out and get back to my roots. Play the kind of music that defined me. I'm sorry, what did you say?"

"Duane and I have been sleeping together," she said matter-of-factly the same way a person would say the sun was shining.

There it was: the one-two-three combination and knock-out. "Excuse me?"

"We wanted to wait and make it official. I had no idea that Duane and the guys were going to replace you. Duane wants me to manage the band."

"Don't you mean Kris with a *K*?"

"In bed he's still Duane."

65

"Of course he is."

"Oh, and can I come over and get my stuff?"

What stuff? All she had in the apartment was her toothbrush and tampons.

Well, that turned out well. As I headed north on Clark, I needed something to take my mind off things and to satisfy my hunger pangs—I hadn't eaten since the previous afternoon. I stopped in at the first place that wasn't crowded, Ahmed's Fantastic Falafel Factory, and ordered a falafel sandwich and a Coke. While I waited for my food, I played back the morning in my mind. From the moment Duane called, it had all been orchestrated so well. He knew that I would go and see Chet first after he called, followed by Cassandra. Duane had it all tied up so neatly. With Chet and Cassandra out of the way, the coup was complete.

I was so distracted trying to make sense out of what was happening, I hadn't paid much attention to the two Asian women seated at a table across from me. However, they had my attention now as they kept on stealing glances at me as I slowly chewed my sandwich.

"You're him, aren't you?" one of the women, the taller and the cuter of the two, finally asked.

"Excuse me?" I said, wiping away a splotch of salad dressing from the corner of my mouth.

"You're him. You're the drummer from Post Nasal Drip," she said, looking at me and then turning to her friend. "See, I told you that it was him."

Finally, there was one bright spot in my shitty day. Fortunately for me, they hadn't heard the news. That's when it suddenly dawned on me that there was no way Duane was going to pull this off. There were a lot of people who wanted to see PND and not whatever evolution or metamorphosis Kris Bermuda and the Triangles had in store later that evening. Drum machines and a catchy new name didn't make a band. News of my demise had been greatly exaggerated.

"Yeah, that's me," I said, sitting up in my chair and tapping the edge of the table with my fingers. It was my signature gesture when someone recognized me as a drummer.

"You guys suck," the woman said as they both got up and walked past my table with a swish of mini-skirt.

I smiled, and considering how lousy my day had been up to this point, took it as a compliment.

Of course, there was one thing I still had to do. I had to see for myself what Duane had done to my band. I wanted to be there when they got laughed or booed off stage. I wanted to walk up to Duane, a.k.a. Kris with a fucking *K* and tell him what a fucking idiot he was. I was in no mood to go back to my apartment, so after I finished my falafel sandwich in peace, I continued my trek up Clark until fate stepped in again.

This time, fate threw a white Subaru with five skinheads from the suburbs, judging from the community college parking sticker on the windshield, in my path. The car nearly ran me over as I prepared to cross the street. Skinheads from the suburbs, I thought; reminded me of that Camper van Beethoven song, "Take the Skinheads Bowling." The driver shot me a dirty look, doing his best Johnny Rotten snarled lip impersonation, but it looked more like the cold pursed lips of a fish. On the rear bumper, I spotted a faded Post Nasal Drip bumper sticker next to another one that read "Bush/Quayle '88."

As I neared 1060 West Addison and Wrigley Field, the traffic got heavy, and the sidewalks grew crowded with pedestrians, mostly Cubs fans on their way to the famous ballpark for the first night game. After years of debate and outrage from baseball purists who still believed that baseball at Wrigley should be played during the day as God had intended (though in the early 1940s, Cubs owner P.K. Wrigley was going to install lights, but donated the lights and stands to the war effort after Pearl Harbor), the current owners finally saw the light. One reason: the owners were threatened that if the Cubs ever reached postseason play, the team would have to play those games in the ballpark of their arch-rivals, the St. Louis Cardinals.

All the major and local networks were covering this historic event, as well as CNN and ESPN; Chicago's WGN was calling the shots, but everyone wanted to get in on history in the making. I could never understand why the Cubs were so popular when the only thing they were good at was losing and making fans wait until next year. Well, now could they break their fans' hearts at night, too.

The significance of the date of the first night game was not lost on me, either—now that I could add getting fired and getting dumped by my girlfriend, and most likely canned from Tommy Jackson's. If you added up the numbers, 8/8/88, they came to thirty-two, which—aside from the temperature that water freezes, the number of teeth in a full set of adult human teeth (I just read about that in *Reader's Digest* the other day) and my age (I turned 32 in May)—was also the year that Jesus was supposedly crucified, which pretty much summed up my day so far.

And as it turned out, Duane's new band was the headline act at The Metro, just up the street from Wrigley. Back when we booked the gig, August 8, was just another day, until we learned a few weeks later, to our chagrin, that the Cubs would be having their first night game on the same date. *Great. Now we have to compete with history and a bunch of lovable losers. Our fans won't be allowed within a ten-block radius of the park.* We had talked about canceling, but the when owner threatened us, telling us that when he was through suing our asses, we'd be lucky getting a gig as street musicians, we decided not to back out. Looking at the chaos and the madness that had descended upon Wrigleyville, I wondered how many people would come out to hear Kris Bermuda and the Triangles. Fate could very well come to my rescue.

The Cubby Bear, a popular watering hole catty-corner from Wrigley, was a full-blown party headquarters as was every other bar and restaurant in the neighborhood. I fought my way through the crowd that had engulfed the area and spread out like an amoeba, swallowing everything in its path. The heat and humidity were unbearable. My T-shirt clung to my body, and sweat dripped from my brow. Most of the Midwest had been in a drought all summer with temperatures soaring into the high eighties and nineties daily. Sweaty fans and tourists decked out in an assortment of Cubs gear, men without shirts and women in bikini tops, precariously balancing and gripping super-sized paper cups filled with beer in outstretched arms, weaved and staggered their way through the crowd.

Police officers barked warnings and announcements through bullhorns and loud-speakers. A string of firecrackers exploded inside a metal trash can. The air reeked of coconut sun tan butter, beer, and cigarette smoke. High overhead, the Goodyear Blimp silently hovered above the spectacle unfolding around the ballpark.

I spotted the same white Subaru with the five skinheads inside being rocked by three beefy Cubs fans who thought anyone in this vicinity ought to be decked out in Cubby blue and driving a Chevrolet from Celozzi-Ettleson.

Good. I hated Illinois skinheads.

With or without me there was a good turnout at the Metro. Obviously, they had been planning this move for weeks. Probably fearing the promoter would find another act, or worse, cancel the show, they waited until the day of the show. Bastards. They had it all figured out. I had bought a baseball cap from a vendor outside to avoid being recognized, pulled it down over my blonde hair, and slipped in surreptitiously through a side door. Once inside, I bought a drink and stood off to one side as the ballroom filled up.

When Duane a.k.a. Kris Bermuda and the retooled Post Nasal Drip, a.k.a. The Triangles, took to the stage, it started out slow. They took minimalism to new heights. The stage was dark and barren except for a projection screen at the front of the stage. The house lights went down and the countdown for the beginning of the movie was projected on the screen. It went down as far as the number two before the screen went to black for a few seconds before the film faded into a white room bathed in light with a Ludwig drum kit in the middle of the room: my drum kit with PND in red letters stenciled on the bass drum head. The film ran for a few seconds with the camera stationary and focused on the drum kit when all of a sudden the drum kit exploded in a flash of pyrotechnics—sparks, flames, smoke, and pieces of the drum flew in the air.

The crowd around me erupted into a frenzied applause.

Those bastards. Those fucking bastards blew up my drum kit!

The stage went dark again when the film stopped. Then, as the screen was raised, a single Fresnel spotlight illuminated the drum machine on a stand at the back of the stage. Somewhere off stage, someone switched it on with a remote. The sound started low, a kick drum, which grew louder and louder until it boomed and reverberated. This was followed by a keyboard sampling of the first chorus of "Take Me Out to the Ballgame" with plenty of echo and reverb.

When the lights finally came up on the stage, eight Fresnel spotlights shining on Duane, Chet, Vince and Dirk hung overhead with four more flood-lights on the stage shining upwards. There was one more surprise: Dirk and Vince had traded in their axes for synthesizers. Only Chet still had his guitar, but he stood behind a Roland synthesizer. They looked more like Kraftwerk wannabes, and I liked those guys. *Fun, fun, fun on the Autobahn.* Well, I knew Kraftwerk (I partied with the band after a show at the Aragon Ballroom), and Duane's new band were no Kraftwerk. What was more disturbing was that no one around me seemed the least bit fazed that Post Nasal Drip was not playing. Duane, a.k.a. Chris with a fucking *K* had pulled off a rock and roll coup.

As soon as they launched into some New Order sounding-like version of "Pretty Woman" a young girl dressed in red and black standing next to me said they were orgasmic and if she had been wearing any panties she would have thrown them on stage.

I wanted to throw up.

The band played just one thirty-minute set of ten songs, but I didn't recognize any of the material. Duane thanked everyone for

70

coming out and supporting them, even the wayward Cub fans who came in out of the rain that had been falling for over an hour, and announced that they would be back again in a month. I could just see the headline in the concert review section of the next *Chicago Reader*: Post Nasal Dropped.

I had seen and heard enough. At the bar in the back of the room, I recognized a familiar face standing off to one side. Even with a Cubs cap pulled down over his head and sunglasses, it was hard not to miss Vic Sneed, who at six-feet-five, towered over the other patrons. Vic was PND's original bassist, but citing artistic integrity and differences, he had quit right before our Chicagofest debut. Now he was waiting on tables at Ed Debevic's and, as he put it, "having the time of his life."

I bought myself a drink and joined Vic at the end of the bar. On a television above the bar, WGN was showing highlights of the first few innings of the game before Mother Nature had her way with the Cubs and the first night game at Wrigley was rained out. *Talk about your irony.*

"I had to see if it was true," Vic said.

"Love the disguise," I said, pointing to his cap and jersey. "You're lucky the bouncer didn't kick you out for impersonating a Cubs fan."

"You're not far off yourself. You're lucky you weren't kicked out for impersonating a drummer," Vic laughed.

"Very funny," I said jabbing him in the ribs.

"Really sorry, man," Vic said. "Who was it, Duane?"

I nodded.

"I never liked that poseur. Remember that time we played at Mabel's in Champaign and one of the guys from REO Speedwagon came in? I've never seen anyone kiss ass faster in my life than Duane did that night," Vic said, looking over his sunglasses at two mini-skirted girls hanging out at the bar near us.

"Cassandra dumped me, too."

"Damn, Tyler, when it rains it pours," Vic said, grinning when he realized the pun he had made.

"I've been looking for a reason to get out of this racket once and for all. Maybe this is a blessing in disguise; maybe it's a sign like night

71

games at Wrigley. It's time to cash in what dreams I have left and move on."

"And you came to this conclusion only after your band fired you and your girlfriend dumped you?" Vic said, tossing back his drink. "Just last month you were boasting how life had never been sweeter."

"Call it an epiphany."

"You know what your problem is, Tyler? You still believe in all this, but the fact is, you're a dinosaur."

On a TV behind the bar, famed Cubs announcer Harry Caray broke the tragic news that the first night game at Wrigley Field had been called on account of rain and that the first night game would have to be played tomorrow. The station showed the same footage of a couple of Cubs players sliding on the blue tarp that covered the infield. If they only showed that much enthusiasm when they were playing, maybe the team would have a winning season. On the other hand, the team was just as popular having one losing season after another. I wouldn't be surprised, in the grand scheme of all things controversial and conspiratorial, if that was what Cubs management wanted all along.

After a recap of the first three innings, including a home run by Ryne Sandberg, the coverage cut to a live shot of the street outside the ballpark where a reporter was interviewing people on the street.

"Although the rain might have ended tonight's historic moment at Wrigley Field, it didn't dampen the spirits of these diehard Cubs fans," the reporter said as the camera panned past a crowd of people yelling and hamming it up for the camera.

In the background, there was no mistaking Duane and Cassandra wearing matching black vinyl raincoats, sharing a red umbrella, and walking briskly down the street as though they were fleeing the scene of an accident.

Next time, Duane. Next time.

After I had parted with Vic, promising to stop in at Ed Debevic's when he was working, I started my trek down Clark. Outside it was a mess as rain-drenched fans sought shelter in bars already overflowing with patrons or headed to the Addison El station or bus stops. The streets and sidewalks were littered with the flotsam of the day's festivities and the rainy debacle at the end. Most of the TV crews had already left; those that stayed behind were treated to drunken renditions of "Take Me Out to the Ballgame" and, for some bizarre but not unrelated reason, "Raindrops Keep Falling on my Head" from fans who refused to go home.

As I walked down Clark, I could see the Sears Tower rising up from the mist. It was a sight I never grew tired of in all the years I lived in the city. There was nothing more romantic than Chicago at night, unless of course, you were kicked out your band and dumped by your girlfriend on the same day.

Further on down, I passed one of the skinheads from the white Subaru. His day hadn't gone so well, either. He was sitting on the curb, holding the steering wheel of his car, watching what was left of it be towed away. From the looks of the debris on the street and sidewalk, he had lost control, driven up on the sidewalk and tried to take out a concrete bench and utility pole. The bench and pole had won. Standing off to one side, a police officer scribbled out an accident report. The skinhead's four cohorts who had abandoned their friend, now waited for a bus across the street.

The skinhead looked up at me with tear-filled eyes; mascara ran down his cheeks. He tilted his head in a quizzical manner as if to say that he recognized me. However, when he did speak, all that he could manage was, "My father's going to kill me."

"Shit happens, pal," I said.

In a sewer opening overflowing with water not far from where this blubbering skinhead sat, I saw a flyer for Kris Bermuda and the Triangles. It spun around in a tiny whirlpool before it was dragged under with all the other debris and flotsam and, like this night, gone forever.

In Autumn, the Ancient Gingko Rains Yellow Tears

There's this photograph I took of you. It was at the end of that chilly, autumn day when we went to Yongmunsa Temple to visit the tallest and biggest gingko tree in Korea. You wore those black leggings, the ones I bought for you at the Lotte Department Store the weekend before, along with your brown leather mini-skirt, the one I loved so much. We were coming down from the temple on our way to the bus stop when I stopped to see how much film I had left in my camera. I know I should have brought more that day, especially how I had gone on and on about wanting to go to one more place before I flew back to the States, but I didn't, and I was down to my last shot. When I looked up, you were about fifty meters ahead of me, your gray coat and long black hair—the hair you promised not to cut when you found out how much I loved it—flowing in the wind. You stopped and turned to see if I was behind you. At that precise moment, the light from the setting sun, reflected from your face in just the right way with this gorgeous red maple in front of you, framing your face. It was beautiful. Pure photographic poetry. I held my breath and slowly pressed the shutter release button. I didn't want to spoil this shot. If nothing else, I wanted this to be a lasting reminder of everything that we had and everything we shared.

I wanted this moment to be about you before it was gone forever.

"According to *Lonely Planet* it's the oldest ginkgo tree in Korea," I said, dog-earing the page of the guidebook for future reference.

Joo-hee held a cup of jujube tea in front of her round face and breathed in the perfume before she sipped the sweet tea. "That's nice."

It was two weeks before I returned to the States to get a new visa for a university job I started in January. Instead of spending the weekend in my apartment, where my roommate, Chet, would most certainly be a nuisance, I was hoping we could find someplace special to go.

The tallest and biggest gingko tree in Korea? There was no way I was going to pass it up.

"We can leave on Friday after we finish work, spend the night, and come back late on Saturday."

Joo-hee pursed her burgundy lips and set the cup of tea down. I could tell she wasn't that enthused about my idea.

"What's wrong with your apartment?" she asked, looking toward the entrance as if she were expecting someone she knew to enter. "Why do we have to go somewhere?"

Ever since my first autumn in Korea, I had been crazy about gingko trees. They were everywhere. We had them back home, in Illinois, but I never noticed them until I came to Korea. Although the smell was enough to gag you when you walked underneath them, in autumn when their leaves turned golden yellow they were a sight to behold; especially on one of those gray, dreary rainy days when the trees shone brightly before the rain and cold stripped them of their fleeting beauty. Koreans loved them just as much; the fallen leaves on certain sidewalks and streets in Seoul were not raked or swept until folks had the chance to enjoy them. One of these streets in Seoul, which ran along the outside of Toksu Palace, was covered with so many fallen leaves that it was often called "The Street of Fallen Leaves."

"I thought it would be neat for us to get away for the weekend," I said. "It's going to be six weeks before I get back here and who knows when we'll be able to go anywhere."

"I suppose we could go," she said wearily. She watched a young couple, probably around our age, sit down at a table next to ours. "If that's what you want."

"Come on," I said, turning on my charm as best as I could. "It'll be fun. Just like it was in the beginning."

I thought I saw a smile form on her lips and her eyes twinkle, but it was only the reflection of a neon sign in the window.

In the beginning, before our world was turned upside down, it was fun.

My best friend, Ken, and his girlfriend, Ji-young, set us up on a blind date six weeks after I had arrived in Korea. It was also Ken who told me that she had this wild streak. I knew she dated a few foreigners in the past, even some Army captain at this military base in Seoul. I knew about her wild vacation in Italy and France where she got arrested for dancing naked in a fountain. It was what attracted me to her in the first place.

However, she wasn't anything like that when we first dated. Although we ended up in bed on our second date, after that we took things slow. We spent our weekends together exploring Seoul—both the well-traveled tourist path of sights and attractions as well as lesser-known, off-the-beaten-path haunts and landmarks. We wandered in the back alleys of Insa-dong, an area known for its antiques and galleries, and spent hours sipping green tea and chewing sweet rice cakes in tiny teahouses that only an inner circle of tea aficionados and well-seasoned travelers knew. Day trips took us to Wolmi-do, an island west of Seoul that was the sight of the Inchon Landing during the Korean War, and Kanghwa Island where we spent a night in a hotel next to one of Korea's oldest temples, which had survived the ravages of the Mongol invasions. During the week, when she had to travel to the southern part of the city for her job, we sometimes met in the afternoon at one of a dozen coffeehouses on a side street not far from where I taught. Named after favorite artists and composers, they were the perfect rendezvous points for our afternoon trysts. Our favorite? Vincent. It had these private booths where we could sit next to each other, hold hands, and sip lemon tea. Soon, we were slipping off to my apartment not far from Olympic Stadium, for two or three hours of carnal delight before we returned to work.

For three months, everything was great. I loved my job. Loved Korea. And I loved Joo-hee.

Then one day, Ken dropped a bombshell.

"Bummer about Joo-hee," Ken said one day while we were on break. Between classes, we would walk up to the roof of the six-story building where we taught to smoke. From here we could see Seoul Tower on top of Mt. Nam in the distance. The horizon was dotted with one sky crane after another. It seemed as though the entire city was one massive construction site.

"What do you mean?" I asked.

"Joo-hee is going to America," Ken added. "Ji-young told me the other day. That's got to suck."

Joo-hee hadn't said anything about going to America. She had talked about wanting to go to Japan, but that was only when she had her next vacation. It felt like someone had sucker-punched me.

"Oh yeah, America," I said, pretending that I knew all about her plans. "She mentioned something about that."

"It's only for a year, so that's not too bad. Unless, of course, you're not here when she gets back," Ken said, smiling. "Well, you know what they say—'there's plenty of fish in the sea.'"

I thought about bringing it up to Joo-hee the next time we were together, but she had other late-breaking news: her father got her a new job that had her traveling between Seoul and Pusan three times a week. Sometimes she stayed overnight instead of taking the train back. Sometimes she spent the weekend with one of her friends.

Although we saw less and less of each other, Joo-hee assured me that this job was only temporary. And at least for the moment, her plans to America were on hold.

"Maybe it's a good thing for us," she said as she snuggled up to me in bed. "Maybe we need to take things slow for a while."

I hurried underneath the city on the green subway line. Getting from the language school I taught at next to Kangnam Subway Station to Kangbyeon Station, where the East Bus Terminal was located, took twenty-five minutes, give or take a couple of minutes at crowded stations like Samseong or Chamsil where the trains emptied most of the riders and took on new ones. However, I had gotten a late start. And to make matters worse, Seoul was being pounded by the remnants of a late-season typhoon.

I got to the bus station with minutes to spare but it was to no avail. Joo-hee, foul mood, and all, was already waiting for me.

"We could have waited until the morning," she said, walking up to me near the gate for the bus. "It's a mess outside."

"Here," I said handing her a bag of warm chestnuts and a can of coffee, which I had picked up for such an emergency. "I figured you could use this."

She smiled and tenderly grabbed my arm the way she did when we first started dating. "Thank you."

We found ourselves a place to sit and waited for our bus. Four noisy U.S. service members passed in front of us. One of them looked at Joo-hee and did a double take before he and his friends were swallowed up by a crowd of middle-aged Korean women in brightly colored jackets.

Although it normally took one hour to reach the town that made a living off all the pilgrims and tourists who came to this temple, given the rain and traffic jam as thousands of people headed to the mountains for the last weekend of autumn foliage, it took over two hours to reach our destination. We found a motel and ordered some chicken from a mom-and-pop shop around the corner. Joo-hee, who still wasn't feeling too well, fell asleep on the bed watching a Korean drama. I walked outside to get some fresh air and sneak a cigarette. The rain had finally stopped. Tomorrow promised to be a perfect day. I grabbed a beer and sat outside a mini mart. A young couple strolled in front of me. The woman was pregnant. My stomach twisted in a knot. It happened every time I saw a pregnant woman. It would have been around this time that Joo-hee and I would have had our baby.

When Joo-hee had told me she was pregnant, there had really been only one thing that I wanted to do. My reaction must have caught her by surprise.

"Wow, that's wonderful," I said, in the same coffeehouse where we had spent many afternoons in each other's arms. "We can do this, right?"

"I can't have the baby," she said. "I'm not ready to start a family. I don't want to end up like girls I know."

We had been very careful. I used a condom most of the times we had sex; the other times Joo-hee counted the days between her last menstrual cycle. However, there was that one time, when we had gone

78

to Shinch'on in the western part of the city and ended up in a love hotel and didn't have time to go looking for condoms at two in the morning. That was probably the night.

"Why didn't you use a condom?" she asked, furrowing her brow. "I don't know what I'm going to do."

She moved away from me on the bench and grabbed a handful of tissue paper. Then we sat silently for a few minutes, drinking lemon tea. In the background "Unchained Melody" played for the thousandth time. The song, which had once been our song, painfully mocked the moment. Her eyes were red and moist.

"What's wrong with starting a family?" I asked. For over a year, since I started teaching, I had been saving a couple hundred dollars a month. It wasn't much, but it was a start. "If I can get a university job when my current contract is over, we'll have more than enough money. Look at my buddy Mike. He and his wife had a baby a year ago and he makes just a little more than I do."

"You don't understand," she sobbed. "It's not that easy."

"It's your father, isn't it?"

She nodded.

For as long as we dated, Joo-hee's father had been the one constant that jeopardized our relationship. He didn't approve of her dating a foreigner, especially an American. Sometimes I thought she dated foreign men just out of spite. On the other hand, her mother was more understanding, hoping that her daughter would find the right man, Korean or foreign, and settle down.

One time she had a fight with her father and moved in with me a few days until things quieted down. However, her father came looking for her, which would have been a real problem had he raised more of a fuss. At six in the morning one Saturday, we were both startled awake by loud banging on my apartment door followed by her father yelling. Joo-hee wrapped a blanket around her body and huddled in the corner. I thought for sure he was going to break the down the door. I was also worried that my next-door neighbor would call the police again—like he did a year ago when a drunken salaryman tried to break down the

79

door because he had gone to the wrong apartment and thought I was inside his apartment with his wife.

Fortunately, my neighbor wasn't home. Her father screamed and yelled, banged and kicked the door a few times before Joo-hee's mother managed to quiet her father down and take him home without any more incident. Joo-hee moved back home that afternoon and we didn't see each other for a month until things cooled down. I thought for sure her father would notify my school. That happened to one teacher who was only at my school for a few months. He also had a run-in with an irate father who didn't care much for foreigners. The teacher was gone in a few days.

But now, everything that had stood in our way of marrying one day paled in comparison.

"Are you sure this is what you want to do?"

Joo-hee bit down on her bottom lip and brushed away the tears from her eyes.

"Yes," she said in a weak voice.

As much as I hated to admit it, Joo-hee was right. We were not ready to start a family.

"I'm going to need some money."

There was a fellow I heard about at my school before I arrived who knocked up his Korean girlfriend and had to pay for her abortion, which of course, was illegal in Korea. Doctors who performed them took a huge risk and their rates reflected this. He ended up having to pay almost one million won, a little over one thousand dollars.

"Of course," I said. "I want to be there with you."

Joo-hee looked away from the table. A few tables across from us another young couple appeared to be having a serious conversation. I wondered what they were talking about.

"No, I don't want you there with me," Joo-hee said. "I have a friend."

"I understand," I said, holding her hand tightly.

We didn't say anything when we walked back to the subway station. I didn't know what else to say. It was only after I watched the train she was on disappearing down the tracks when I realized that I hadn't said I was sorry.

It took us almost thirty minutes to reach the temple entrance; the tree was located near the back of the temple grounds. Joo-hee and I had been to a lot of temples in Korea, but each time I went to one, it was like the first time. I got all giddy and excited, like a kid on Christmas morning.

It was a delightfully chilly autumn morning. I loved this time of the year in Korea when Korea's rugged beauty was delineated by a cold, cobalt sky that seemed to go on forever. Koreans liked to brag about how beautiful their autumns were, and I agreed. It was the kind of day that I wished I could bottle up to open whenever I wanted.

However, there weren't many people in the temple. If the tree was anything like it was described in my Korea guidebook, the temple should have been crawling with visitors. As it was, we passed a group of *ajummas*, middle-aged Korean women in colorful hiking gear. A few of them, when they saw me, said "MacGyver" and then started laughing. Ever since I arrived in Korea, my pale complexion and shaggy ginger hair had many Koreans comparing me to the Richard Dean Anderson character. *MacGyver* was a very popular show in Korea when I arrived; in fact, it was so popular, Koreans started calling a Swiss Army Knife a "MacGyver" because Anderson's character was so ingenious on the show. I certainly didn't mind the comparison. I got a lot of mileage out of it.

One of the women grabbed Joo-hee's arm and jabbered away about one thing or another. When the woman looked at me again, she smiled before she caught up with her friends.

"What did she say?" I asked.

"She asked if we were married," Joo-hee replied.

"What did you say?"

"Not yet."

I smiled.

It took us another fifteen minutes to finally reach the tree. Whatever euphoria I had been feeling earlier quickly disappeared. The tree was bare. Only a few leaves, which had survived the hard rain and cold, fluttered at the top. The muddy ground was carpeted with damp, yellow leaves. I stood there, my hands on my hips, and camera dangling from my neck. I shook my head.

"I'm sorry," Joo-hee said. "I guess we were too late."

"There's always next year, right?" I said, trying to make the most of the situation.

Joo-hee smiled. "Yes, there's always next year."

Six months after she had had the abortion, there were emotional and spiritual scars that were going to take time to heal. I gave her as much time and distance as she needed, but in those six months, that wasn't always possible. Just when I thought we were getting back to what we once had, she drifted away. Part of it was her new job, which took her away more and more, as well as her on-and-off again troubles with her father. And part of it was that she couldn't forgive me for getting her pregnant in the first place.

Before the abortion, I called her every night before I went to bed. No matter if either one of us had gone out with our colleagues, we always found time to talk. I still called her at night, but not as much as before.

"When can we see each other?" I had asked one of those nights when she was more talkative than usual. Her new boss complimented her on a pair of high heels she had bought at a boutique in Myong-dong. He told her that he liked the way she walked in them.

"Not yet," she said. "I need more time. I hope you understand."

And I gave her more time and space.

One afternoon I bumped into her at the KOEX Center in central Seoul. I was walking out of the subway station when I saw her and a man who I took for one of her male colleagues walking in the opposite direction.

"Joo-hee!" I yelled.

Either she didn't hear me amidst the din of the subway station or had and didn't want to acknowledge because she was with one of her colleagues. I cut across the throng of commuters and shoppers and caught up with her.

"Hey, Joo-hee," I said, out of breath.

"Oh, hi," she said with a sheepish expression.

I couldn't tell if she was more embarrassed that I had bumped into her or that she didn't know whether she should introduce her male friend. She looked good. She was wearing her hair long again like she did when we first met. With everyone feeling a little uncomfortable, I provided the exit strategy.

"Call me, okay?" I said.

"Yeah, sure," she said as she continued towards the subway entrance with her friend.

I waited to see whether she would turn and look back, but a train having just arrived below, immediately filled the subway station with a dense, fast-moving mass heading out of the station.

We had dinner in a family restaurant that afternoon before we headed back to Seoul. We were the only customers. We warmed ourselves in front of a barrel that burned *yontan*, a cylinder-shaped briquette about the size of a can of motor oil. The mother played with a small child in her lap. I could see the pain and guilt in Joo-hee's eyes as she watched the child tug at her mother's hair. When the child saw me, she walked toward me and fell into my arms. I bounced the child on my knee.

"You're good with children," the mother said in Korean.

I looked across the table at Joo-hee. The steam from the bubbling bowl of kimchi stew rose up in front of her face.

"Joo-hee, I'm sorry," I said.

"I know," she said.

At the bus terminal, while we waited for our bus back to Seoul, we watched an elderly couple help each other across the cold, drafty room. The man, his face worn and tired, gently tugged at his wife's long gray overcoat as they shuffled across the cold concrete floor. In my heart, I wanted to say that someday that would be us, but it probably wouldn't have made any difference.

The following Friday, after I turned in my final student grades and said goodbye to everyone, Joo-hee and I went to Kimpo Airport in the western part of the city. I would be flying to Portland and then to Dallas.

"Six weeks is not a long time," I said, sipping a Coke in a lounge on the second floor.

She nodded.

"I'll call you when I get to Texas," I said.

Overhead, a loudspeaker announced that the flight to Portland would be boarding soon.

"That's my flight," I said, grabbing my carry-on bag.

We didn't say anything as we walked downstairs and stopped in front of the immigration control point.

"Well, this is it," I said. "Talk to you soon."

She nodded. "Have a safe trip.

"See you soon," I said. "I love you."

I put my arms around her; however, she backed off a little, embarrassed that people were watching us, before she allowed me the hug. She was wearing the perfume that I bought for her last month. It would be a fragrance that would soon be a bittersweet reminder of this moment in time.

"I love you, too," she finally said.

I gently kissed her on the cheek, looked into her eyes one last time, and walked toward the immigration official. After I showed my passport and started for the entrance into immigration, I turned around for one last look, but Joo-hee had already left.

It was a few weeks before I got around to developing that last roll of film in the camera. There were lots of shots of Joo-hee striking her best Madonna or Mariah Carey pose; one of her sticking her tongue out at me; one of her looking

84

moody as we waited for the bus to leave Seoul. I thumbed through all the photos, but the one, the one photograph of her running down the mountain and the sun's setting rays just catching her just right, wasn't among them. That's too bad. I guess I didn't have enough film in the camera after all.

The Roads We Must Travel

Kim Kyung-sook stood on the shore of the frozen, ancient river and pondered the fate that had brought her to this most desolate and dangerous location. Wrapped in layers of threadbare rayon and vinylon clothing, she peered across the river and hoped that she wouldn't have to wait too long. After traveling for more than a day and a half, she had waited a full day more to make sure there would be no soldiers patrolling this part of the river, which also meant that she could not light a fire for fear of being spotted. Hungry and cold, the woman had covered herself up as best she could with an old blanket she had found. Perhaps another person who had come here for the same reason had used the same blanket.

She felt the small bundle under her layer of clothes. Its weight and shape were both comforting and deadly. The man who had given her the bundle told her where to make contact with the Chinese traders who relied on desperate people such as Kyung-sook who would risk everything for the money they would receive in return for the contents: crystal meth. She knew the risks if she were caught: she would either be shot on the spot by one of the patrols or, worse, arrested and sent to one of the work camps where she would most assuredly die soon after. Deeply in debt and not knowing the fate of her husband, who had been sent to one of the work camps for stealing a bag of rice, she did it out of necessity. The risk was definitely worth it if she wanted her family to make it through another severe winter faced with fuel and food shortages.

Getting the drug was easy. In her village there was a man who made it in his kitchen. He had once been a renowned chemist at one of the state-run labs, but when the country fell on hard times and many chemists found themselves out of work, they turned to alternative means to support themselves. There were others who made the drug, but this man was the most reliable. He lost his wife last winter. He didn't care what happened to himself anymore. The government threatened to crack down on the production and sale of crystal meth, but these kitchen labs and the thriving black market along the border between North Korea and China were impossible to stop.

Like many of the people in her village, she had tried the drug she would soon hand off to the Chinese trader. Villagers who had used the drug described how in small quantities it could suppress one's appetite. At first, she wanted nothing to do with it. However, she soon changed her mind. When food was scarce, she gave her eleven-and twelve-year-old sons some of the drug. She knew it was wrong, but their cries at night for something to eat were too much for her to endure. The drug also had other medicinal benefits. She had sometimes taken small amounts for headaches. There were some people in her village who took it as a cure for depression. Everyone who tried it more than once said that once you did use it, it was very hard to stop.

The woman was not the only person in her village who sold the drug to Chinese traders. There were others who were willing to take the risks. Not everyone was so lucky. There was one woman whose son was arrested for smuggling the drug into China. One of the guards then turned around and told her that if she ever wanted to see her son alive again, she had to bring him two grams of the drug. She did, and her son was freed. Another woman was caught and never heard from again.

However, there was another reason why she risked her life and the lives of her children. The woman heard other villagers talking about how if you sold enough of the drug you could afford passage into China and from there south to Laos or Thailand and freedom.

There were rumors that the government wanted to produce the drug again. That's what had happened the last time when the government needed money. If the government started producing the drug again, she might never be able to help her family escape to freedom.

It never crossed her mind that what she was doing was wrong. When she was a young woman, she had been mesmerized by her county's charismatic leader. Once, while she was serving in the army, the leader's son visited her radar station on a mountain. She and the other women in her unit wept when he stopped to talk to them and pose for a photograph. It was one of the happiest days of her life. She believed in her country's policy of *Juche*, or self-reliance. However, not everyone felt the same way that she did. People grew tired of the food shortages and the empty slogans that told them to grow more mushrooms or annihilate the enemy to the last man. These slogans did not improve their lifestyle or put more food on the table. Soon, she dreamed of a better life.

Kyung-sook put a wrinkled, worn hand on her forehead and scanned the rocky shore and the frozen expanse in front of her. It had sounded so easy, four weeks earlier, when the man who had given her the drugs told her what to do. Suddenly she saw a dark figure moving across the frozen river from the opposite shore. She squinted hard, hoping to recognize the figure as best she could. The figure got about halfway across the river—that was the signal for Kyung-sook to walk out on the frozen river and walk toward the middle to meet the man.

She kept a close watch on the shore just in case any patrols suddenly appear, but even if they did, there would be nothing that she could do. Once she had stepped onto the frozen river, there was no turning back. She stepped gingerly on the snow-covered frozen river. The wind howled across the jaundiced sky. Her legs ached with each labored step. A thin layer of ice beneath the snow cracked under her weight. Her breathing was short and irregular as she continued carefully across the frozen expanse before her.

When she got within ten yards of the figure, who turned out to be a middle-aged man dressed in a bulky dark brown overcoat, he gestured toward her to show the bundle. No words needed to be spoken. The transaction was simple. Kyung-sook nodded, retrieved the bundle from inside her coat, and held it up for the man to see. The man nodded and motioned for her to come forward. She slowly approached the trader and handed him the bundle. The trader carefully looked inside and inspected the product to make sure the woman had not duped him. He had done business with other people from her village; he knew the quality of the product and the price that it would fetch.

Satisfied with the product the woman had brought, he shoved the bundle inside his jacket and retrieved a small packet of bills. Just as the trader did by inspecting the product, the woman looked into the packet and counted the bills. When she was satisfied, she nodded, turned, and started back toward the shore. They would meet again in a month.

Kyung-sook caught her breath once she reached the shore. She turned around and saw that the trader had already disappeared behind a hill on the other side of the river. Her stomach ached from having no food; she wished she had kept a little of the drug for herself to ward off the pangs of hunger. However, soon she would have something to eat; soon her whole family would have something to eat. There was a chicken in the butcher's shop that she would buy. Her children would once again know the taste of rice instead of barley. She would stretch this money as much as she could until she could make another trip. Soon, there would be no cries of hunger from her children.

For the first time since she embarked on this journey, she felt a great burden lifted from her soul.

As she started back up the road, the wind whipped across the fallow paddies. Frozen dust and chaff peppered and stung her ruddy face. She wrapped her tattered, threadbare scarf around her face to shield it from the wind and dust as best she could. There was no time to rest. It was imperative that she get off this road as soon as possible.

She traveled about a kilometer when she spotted a truck speeding toward her. She put her hand to her forehead, squinting her eyes for a better look. It was one of the patrols. In the back of the olive drab truck, which had a bright red star on the door, three soldiers clutching automatic weapons bounced up and down. Her heart started pounding. Had they seen her when she walked out on the frozen river? Although she was far away enough from the river as not to draw too much suspicion, to be out here alone on the road wasn't good either. Surely they would stop and question her. She shifted the packet of money under her clothes and continued to walk up the road.

In the distance, she spotted smoke rising from a small farmhouse. That would be her story if asked. She would tell the soldiers that she was on her way to visit a family member who was ill.

When the truck finally reached her, two of the soldiers in the back jumped off and approached the woman. The other soldier in the back trained his weapon on her. There were two more soldiers inside the cab. The two soldiers who approached the woman were young. Their dark green uniforms hung limply on their thin frames. They appeared to be happy to have come across the woman; at the very least, they had something to do to take their mind off the bitter cold.

"Identity card, please," the taller of the two soldiers demanded.

Kyung-sook dug for her card inside her layers of clothes and handed it to the soldier, who furrowed his brow as he examined the details of the card. He looked at Kyung-sook's face and her photograph on the card, back and forth, three times before he was satisfied.

"What are you doing here?" he asked, handing back her identity card. "Don't you know this is a restricted area?"

Kyung-sook shook her head and glanced toward the farmhouse in the distance.

"I'm visiting a friend," she said, pointing to the farmhouse. "She's very ill."

"No one lives in that house," the soldier said. "You're lying."

"Excuse me, Comrade Lee," the other soldier said, stepping forward. "I know this woman."

Kyung-sook slowly lifted her head and looked at the soldier who had just spoken. A smile formed on her lips when she recognized the soldier from her village. She knew his parents. They were good people. The taller soldier, impatient with the proceedings, crinkled his pudgy red nose.

"Search her!" the taller soldier ordered.

"I need to search you, Comrade Kim," the soldier from her village said. His voice was warm and smooth as the sweet bean paste she once enjoyed as a child. "It's okay. I won't hurt you."

The soldier shifted his weapon on his shoulder and reached inside Kyung-sook's overcoat. His hands were cold but soft as he patted the layers of clothing she wore. His hands stopped short of the packet containing the money. Kyung-sook gritted her teeth and tried not to telegraph her fear.

The taller soldier looked on with an amused smile on his face as he watched his comrade search Kyung-sook. When it was obvious that she was harmless, he climbed into the back of the truck.

"*Kapshida!*" the taller soldier said. "Let's go!"

"You need to get off this road," the younger soldier said. "It's too dangerous for someone like you."

When the soldier removed his hands from inside Kyung-sook's overcoat, he accidentally knocked free the packet of money, which fell to the ground. Her eyes widened with fear as she stared at the packet and then at the soldier. Some of the bills were visible. The young soldier looked down at the money and kicked it with his dusty boot.

"What's this?" he asked.

Kyung-sook stared at the packet again and then the soldier. Her eyes traveled to the back of the truck where the other two soldiers waited.

"You need to be more careful, Comrade Kim," the soldier said, reaching down and grabbing the packet. "As I said, this road can be *very* dangerous."

She closed her eyes and waited for the metallic click of a round chambered in one of the weapons and the report of the weapon that would take her life, but neither came. Instead, she heard the shrill laughter of the three soldiers waving her money in the air as the truck bounced down the road leaving in its wake a cloud of dust and black smoke. Kyung-sook's eyes wept from the cold that stung her face as she watched the truck disappear behind a hill.

And for the second time that day, Kyung-sook pondered her fate as she turned and slowly headed home where not even the howling wind could drown out the cries of her children she already heard inside her head.

Maid-Rite

Just down the street from Mike's Sunoco Station the ancient diner—its white, weathered clapboard sides a peeled and faded reminder of better days—was open for lunch with regulars already in place. Seated elbow to elbow around the scarred and stained Formica top counter on wobbly stools that had long since stopped swiveling, the lunch crowd chattered about the weather, politics, and the economy.

Sam Rizzo, the owner, stirred a pan of the crumbled beef for the diner's specialty sandwich and namesake, which was the only thing keeping the diner open. A white chef's cap was pushed back on his bald, oversized head, which was proportional to the body grown rotund from years of neglect and too much beer. His thick arms were covered with nautical tattoos of mermaids, anchors, rudders, and Hawaiian hula girls he got from his time in the Navy during Vietnam. The one of a hula girl on the inside of his right forearm—a reminder of some drunken, exotic port call—was never the subject of scrutiny or debate, unless one asked him to tell the story again about why he had been forced to go back to the tattooist the next day and have her breasts painfully covered.

Outside a line stretched from the main entrance, around the corner, underneath the simple blue sign that advertised "Eat" to the parking lot in back. It was a simple menu that they came for: a Maid-Rite sandwich—finely ground beef cooked and piled on a plain bun, sometimes referred to as a loose meat or tavern sandwich, served with mustard, pickles or chopped onions. At lunch time, the sandwich came with a bag of chips and a Coke on the side. No one would have ever thought about putting ketchup on a Maid-Rite. Not only would that be sacrilegious and a faux pas in Maid-Rite lore, but also because most Maid-Rite purists considered that to be low-class.

And just to prove that he was a good sport in all culinary fairness for the unsuspecting customer who wandered in after getting a whiff of the meat cooking, Sam kept a bottle of ketchup on the counter for emergency purposes, but with a stern warning for anyone who dared to defy tradition. In the twenty years he had the restaurant, no one dared.

"I've been coming here for 15 years," one patron said to another, as he chewed the last of his sandwich and licked his fingers. "Best darn sandwiches in McDonough County."

Bonnie, the waitress behind the counter, nodded and took another order. She blew a wisp of her red hair, which had swept down from her forehead. What's tradition and history got to do with it, she thought when she was making three-fifty an hour plus tips and barely making ends meet? It was only a sandwich, for crying out loud. She tried one once, after having been cajoled by Sam—"If you're going to work here, you better know what one tastes like"—and found the sandwich rather bland, sort of like a sloppy joe without the sauce. If she had it her way, she would have doused it with some of that ketchup.

"Sam, you never disappoint," George Jansen, the chief of police, said, patting his stomach, which hung over his loose-fitting trousers. "Without a question your sandwiches are the best eats in town."

"You know my motto, 'If it's made right, it's gotta be good'," Sam said, turning away from the stove.

Bonnie smiled and rolled her blue eyes as she removed a dirty plate and a quarter left by the previous customer. As long as those quarters added up every day, she could live with Sam's witticisms.

As she continued to work her way along the inside of the counter clearing away the plates, heavy ceramic coffee mugs, and red plastic glasses, the old brass bell above the door sounded as the door swung open and then slammed shut. Bonnie looked up and watched Henry Taylor slowly walk in and sit alone again at the end of the counter. This was the fifth time in as many weeks since she started working here that she noticed him come in after the lunch crowd thinned out and sit on the same stool at the far end of the diner. She couldn't recall him speaking more than two or three sentences to whoever sat close to him, though Sam appeared to know him quite well. Whenever Henry came into the diner, Sam stopped whatever he was doing to welcome him with a nod and a smile.

Henry had snow-white hair and a matching white mustache with twisted ends which accentuated his hollow cheekbones. He had pale blue eyes, the color of a robin's eggs. He looked distinguished and always dressed nicely. The first time Bonnie saw him she thought he must have been a professor at Western Illinois University at one time, or maybe he was a doctor, or a lawyer. She was close: he had taught high school history for thirty years.

Henry always ordered two sandwiches but only ate one of them. Although she already knew the answer, having asked him each time he had been in before, she still asked him whether he would like to have the one he hadn't eaten wrapped up to take home.

"No, that's okay, miss," he said, dabbing the corners of his mouth with a napkin. "Thanks so much for asking."

Bonnie nervously glanced at her watch. She had just enough time to pick up her daughter at the day care center and spend some time with her before she started her second job at Walmart. When she set her handbag on the edge of the counter to hurry things along, she accidentally knocked it off, spilling the contents across the floor. Henry retrieved some of them for her, including her keys attached to an octagonal plastic keychain that contained a photograph of Bonnie, her husband, Steve, and their daughter, Sarah, taken a few days before he deployed to Afghanistan.

"That's a nice photo. I've got a granddaughter about your age," he said, "though it's been a while since we've last seen each other."

"My grandparents died when I was very young," Bonnie said, quickly scooping up the contents of her handbag.

"That's too bad," Henry said, taking one more look at the photo before handing the keychain to Bonnie. "You have a fine-looking family there."

"Thank you," Bonnie said, shoving all the items back into her handbag. "I don't mean to be rude or anything, but I've got to pick up my daughter at daycare and—"

"No need to apologize," Henry said, slowly getting up from the stool.

Bonnie lived in a small three-room apartment on West Adams Street just off the town square. Although small and run-down, it was all she could afford at the time. Besides, it was close enough to work, and her babysitter, Sally, lived in the apartment below. After she had picked up Sarah, they had an hour to have some quality time together before she had to go to Walmart.

"Mommy, did Daddy like chocolate chip cookies as much as I do?" Sarah asked, looking up at her mother with big green eyes. She might have had her mother's red hair and nose, but she definitely had her father's eyes.

They sat together on the floor playing with some colored wooden building blocks waiting for the babysitter to arrive. Bereavement counselors had told her that there might be a delayed reaction to Steve's death for Sarah and that instead of asking about how he died, Sarah, who barely knew her father when he left for Afghanistan, might want to know who he was.

Bonnie looked at her daughter and smiled sadly. She brushed a lock of red hair from her daughter's freckled forehead. "Yes, he did. He liked them a lot."

Sarah smiled. "Can we make some chocolate chip cookies?"

"Sure, we can make some."

Her daughter smiled again as she stacked three blocks on top of one another. Whereas Bonnie was making sure she was doing all she could to help Sarah deal with the loss of her father, she wasn't doing all that good herself. Almost two years after his Humvee hit an IED in Afghanistan, Bonnie still couldn't accept the fact that Steve was gone. She sometimes still woke up in the middle of the night, thinking that she heard the phone ringing and that Steve would be on the other end, alive and well, telling her that it had been a terrible mistake for the Army to tell her that he had been killed in action.

And then she would sit at the kitchen table or in the living room and go through their photo album for the millionth time touching each photo, remembering every moment they spent together.

If he were here he would tell her not to worry and that things would get better with time. He would tell her to be strong and to have faith. That's what she always loved about him. He always knew what to say to make her feel better.

It wasn't only the pain in her heart that she carried with the loss of her husband; it was also the guilt.

For days after 9-11, when the whole nation walked around shocked and numb, Steve talked about how useless he felt sitting around and doing nothing until he decided to join the Army.

"It's only for three years. This is something that I have to do," Steve told her the day he decided to enlist. "Larry and Mark have already enlisted."

"What about our baby?" Bonnie said, rubbing her swollen belly. She was in her third trimester. "What if something happens to you—"

"Nothing is going to happen to me," Steve said, putting an arm around his wife.

"Oh!" Bonnie said.

"What, darling?" Steve asked in an alarmed tone.

"She kicked again!" Bonnie said smiling. She took Steve's right hand and placed it on her belly. "See?"

Steve leaned over and rested his head on her belly. He felt a tiny nudge and movement inside. He turned his head and smiled as he gazed at his wife. "I feel her, too."

Bonnie smiled and ran a hand softly through his blonde hair. She believed him. Everything was going to be fine.

The Vietnam Memorial came to town over the weekend. All two hundred and fifty-two feet of it with its fifty-eight thousand two hundred twenty-five silk-screened names on black, Plexiglas panels half the size of the one in Washington.

A ten-man crew set it up in Chandler Park across the street from the train station; the grass in front of it was already trampled from the procession of people who had been filing by solemnly since last evening and again this morning; in some places, muddy patches—because of the rain that had been falling in the morning—had already appeared.

Moving from east to west, from 1959 to 1975, some people stopped to read or touch a name on the cold, wet panels. Others bowed their heads and said a prayer. Many simply filed by, not sure what they were supposed to do or say. Those who did speak whispered just a hush below the soft undulating spatter of rain upon umbrellas.

At the base of one of the panels, someone left a small teddy bear, its brown body soggy and limp with plastic eyes glistening in the rain. Two panels down, someone else left a framed photograph of two young boys. Brightly colored flowers left in bunches here and there along the wall, accentuated the dark plastic panels and the gray sky overhead.

"Happens all the time," a grizzled, whiskered man in a faded red VFW cap said, warming his hands with a cup of coffee underneath a canopy set up by the Woman's Auxiliary. "I hear there's even a special museum for all the stuff people have left behind."

Men who had been to places like Guadalcanal, Normandy, Bastogne, Peleliu, Chosin, Khe Sanh, and Baghdad—far-away places where their brothers bled and died—men who carried their own personal museums in the scars that ran deep through their souls, nodded their heads in solemn affirmation. Then these men watched one of their own—a father and his son stop along the wall. Together father and son wiped away beads of rain and searched for one name among them all as they gazed at their own silent reflections.

Bonnie, who had cut across the park on her way to the diner, saw Henry out of the corner of her eye talking to some of the men gathered under the canopy. She had heard about the wall from a customer at the diner and wanted to see for herself. Bonnie was both mesmerized and shocked by its solemn presence and the procession of people who slowly moved from one end of the wall to the other. She shuddered when a man walked past her, tears rolling down his puffy, pale cheeks.

She watched Henry slowly walk out from underneath the canopy and move through the sea of bobbing umbrellas toward the wall. He was too old to have been in the war, Bonnie thought as Henry walked to one of the middle panels, touched the cold plastic, and bowed his head.

Two elderly women sharing an umbrella, who had stopped behind Bonnie, watched Henry locate one of the cold names. One of the women turned to the other and asked, "Where did they put all the bodies?"

The following Tuesday was a holiday, Veterans Day, and Bonnie couldn't find a babysitter, so she was forced to bring Sarah to the diner. Bonnie brought along some crayons and paper for Sarah to keep her occupied until she finished her shift. She promised Sam that Sarah wouldn't be a bother. Sam fixed up a special sandwich for Sarah and didn't mind when she asked for some ketchup.

Right on schedule, a little after 1:00, Henry entered the diner and sat on his usual stool. Two patrons, who knew Henry, looked in his direction and silently nodded their heads. Bonnie also glanced at Henry as he sat down, and smiled. *He looks more tired today.* She picked up the two sandwiches for Henry and brought them to him.

"I saw you at the memorial in Chandler Park the other day," Bonnie said, setting the two plates in front of him.

"I've been to the one in Washington, and I saw this one when it came here the first time in 1987," Henry said slowly. "Until you see those names up close, one has no idea of its emotional power."

Bonnie nodded. She felt the same way, but for her it was not just the names, but all those loved ones attached to the names.

"I lost my boy in Vietnam," Henry said, his eyes cloudy with tears. "He was ten days shy of his nineteenth birthday."

"I'm sorry," Bonnie said, sitting down on a stool next to Henry.

98

"When Danny was a boy, we used to come here once a week for a sandwich. I would sit here, and Danny would sit where you are now. The last time was right before he shipped out. At first, I couldn't even come to this part of town. Then slowly over time, I came back here. It was my way of remembering him and the last time we shared a moment together."

Bonnie gasped when she realized why he always ordered two sandwiches and left one untouched.

"Today would have been his sixtieth birthday," Henry said.

Bonnie could feel the pain swelling in her chest; her heart beat faster as she softly sobbed. "That's such a sad story. I'm so sorry for your loss, Mr. Taylor."

"Henry."

Bonnie wiped away the tears from her face.

"Who's this cute-looking girl?" Henry asked, looking down at Sarah as she colored in a sun in the sky.

"Sarah," she said, choosing a green crayon to start coloring the trees.

"Sarah. That's a pretty name," Henry said.

"My daddy picked my name," Sarah, said as she colored in more of a tree.

"What are you drawing, Sarah?" Henry asked.

"A picture of Mommy, Daddy and me," Sarah said, sticking her tongue out the corner of her mouth as she concentrated on making sure she colored the trees correctly. "Daddy's waiting for us here. Right, Mommy?"

Henry looked up at Bonnie with a confused look on his face.

"I lost my husband in Afghanistan two years ago this Friday," Bonnie said in a hushed tone.

Henry looked at Bonnie the same way the veterans had looked at each other in Chandler Park. He took hold of Bonnie's hand, and the two of them sat quietly at the counter and watched Sarah finish her drawing. Sam brought them two cups of coffee, and as Bonnie sat there with Henry and her daughter, for the first time in a very long time, she didn't feel alone.

Mojave Green

All I wanted after pulling my sixth consecutive twelve-hour shift on the flight line was to crawl into bed and sleep for a week, but I couldn't. Instead, I lay in bed staring at the cracked, yellowed ceiling and wondered why my wife's first husband was coming to visit.

No sooner had I arrived home an hour earlier and gotten undressed than Betsy told me that Mitch was in town and wanted to see her.

The window fan rattled as it nudged the last of the cool night air across the room. Outside, the wind hissed through a Joshua tree. In the distance, a peal of thunder rolled across the desert as a few F-4 fighters took off—probably some of the ones that I'd worked on last night.

I grabbed a crumpled pack of Marlboros from the nightstand and stuck one in my mouth. "When?"

"He didn't say." Betsy sat down on the edge of the bed. She brushed a wisp of blonde hair off her freckled forehead. "Sometime today."

She stared out a window that faced the desert toward the air base. Another F-4 took off; the roar of the engine as the afterburner kicked in rippled in the sky overhead Adelanto, the town we lived in near the base.

"He doesn't know we're married."

I snickered low enough for Betsy not to hear me and rolled my eyes.

"I don't think you should be here when he stops by."

"Why didn't you tell him that you don't want to see him?"

"He says he wants to talk. It's the least I could do." She stood and moved over to the closet. "I don't have anything nice to wear."

She pulled out a powder-blue cotton print dress and held it up. I bought that dress for her in San Diego last month. She complained that it made her look too fat. She hung it back up and searched for something else to wear.

"You look fine."

"I don't want him to see me like this."

I stared at the tight yellow shorts and white halter-top she was wearing. The shorts rode high on her butt. Maybe I didn't want him to see her like this.

"Throw on a pair of jeans."

"They're all dirty." She rooted through a pile of clothes at the side of the bed and threw some of the clothes onto the bed. Near the bottom, she pulled out a pair of faded jeans. "You're acting calm about this. When he finds out—"

I cut her off. "He's going to find out sooner or later. He's got at least one friend in the squadron."

"You don't know him. He's probably been drinking. He would never come back here unless he's been drinking."

I did know the way he got, especially the drinking, the gambling, and the fighting. Redlined for promotion three times; at least two Article 15s that I knew of. I knew him by name only—he had been assigned to a different section, but no one that I knew in the squadron ever spoke well of him. He was always in up to his ass with the Security Police, our CO, the first sergeant, and the other crew chiefs.

Once, at the NCO Club, I walked in just after one of his escapades: he had started a fight with some crew chief that I worked with, and it got ugly quick—broken chairs, a table, and a mirror behind the bar. I probably could have gotten in a few punches had I gotten there earlier. It had to be broken up by the Security Police, who ended up hauling five guys away.

Betsy didn't tell me much about him, except that they had had some problems and that she often felt sorry for him. Six months after he was sent overseas, Betsy filed for a divorce. Three months later, we were dating.

The thought of him making a scene entered my mind. "Maybe I should hang around."

"No, that's okay. He won't try to pull any shit." She took off her halter-top and slipped on a bra. "Maybe you can drive into base or town."

"Just let me get a few hours of sleep." I stretched out on the bed and stared at the ceiling. There weren't these many cracks in the ceiling when we moved in here a few months ago, but then that was before the new runway was built—before the fighters started to take off and land over our apartment.

In the next room I heard Betsy singing a song by the group Journey. I grabbed another pillow on the bed and scrunched it over my head to drown out the singing.

I hated Journey, and she knew that.

I woke up sweating. I glanced at the clock on the dresser. Eleven o' clock. Three hours of sleep. What the hell was I going to do on base? Well, at least I didn't have to go into work. After pulling six straight twelve-hour shifts, I had the next two days off.

After I splashed some cold water on my face and brushed my teeth, I felt better. I finished a cigarette before I slipped into a pair of jeans and a T-shirt and walked out into the living room. Betsy worked a broom across the worn, faded black and white checked linoleum floor, stirring up a cloud of dust as I shuffled toward the sofa. She played it safe and opted for jeans and a Black Sabbath T-shirt. I approved. Lipstick, rouge, and blue eye shadow completed her ensemble. Just last week she had complained that it was too hot to bother with makeup. I reached underneath the sofa and grabbed my sneakers. I glanced up at Betsy as she passed with the broom. Nail polish.

Betsy caught me staring at her. "I don't want him to think—"

I waved her off. I was in no mood to get into it with her. "I'll be back in a few hours."

She intercepted me halfway toward the door. "You knew there was the chance this would happen."

I looked past Betsy to the screen door.

Betsy grabbed my arm. "I've dreaded this day, too."

She kissed me on the cheek but tried not to smudge her lipstick.

I stopped before I reached the screen door. A rusted brown pickup truck came to a halt right in front of our apartment. As a cloud of dust settled around the truck, a tall and lean man climbed out. Standing up straight, he stretched and pushed his aviator sunglasses up his sunburned nose. He reached down to straighten faded jeans over scuffed brown boots with thin arms covered with tattoos. He ran a hand through oiled hair and worked up a gob of mucus from his throat which he spat into the sand in front of him.

I backed away from the door just as Betsy saw the truck and Mitch. The way his body jerked and swaggered as he walked up the sidewalk reminded me of one of those Komodo lizards.

Mitch rapped hard on the screen door and peered in through the door over his sunglasses. Betsy took a deep breath and exhaled slowly before she opened it. They stood in front of each other for a few awkward seconds before Mitch finally leaned in to attempt a hug. Betsy stood in front of Mitch with her arms at the side and allowed him to put his arms around her before she backed away a few steps. Awkward was perhaps an understatement. The two of them reminded me of two kids at a school dance attempting to slow dance for the first time— neither one wanting to be the first one to make a move but hoping the other one would.

Mitch removed his sunglasses and surveyed the apartment. "Place looks the same." He retrieved a toothpick from behind his left ear and stuck it into his mouth as he walked past Betsy.

"Mitch, this is—"

"I know." Mitch reeled around and stuck out his hand. "Can't keep secrets around here."

He rolled off a dry laugh that was part snort, part cackle.

I shook his hand, but withdrew it quickly, as if I'd touched a dead fish. "I was on my way out."

104

"Nice to meet you, dude." Mitch plopped down on the sofa and stretched out his legs over the coffee table. "Yessir, this place hasn't changed."

"I'll be okay," Betsy whispered.

Outside, as I walked toward our Toyota, I heard them laugh. I wondered if I shouldn't stay.

Even though I knew Betsy had been married to Mitch when we first started seeing each other, it wasn't until our wedding night in Vegas that she told me about the divorce. There we were, getting ready to consummate our marriage, as if it needed any consummating, when she told me all about the divorce. She told me how she took off for Tijuana with her best friend, who had just gone through a divorce there, and recommended the same attorney—some storefront divorce attorney named Rodriquez. It took thirty minutes and four hundred dollars. Betsy never did tell me why Mitch didn't contest. And I never bothered to ask.

"He's out of our lives now," Betsy assured me, as she snuggled up next to me in bed in our hotel next to the airport. "He'll never bother us."

Banging a guy's wife while he was on deployment was one thing, but stealing her away from the poor sucker was an entirely different set of circumstances. I felt a little uncomfortable at first when Betsy told me all these "details"—not that they would have made any difference, but it would have been nice to know before we said "I do" at the Silver Bell Wedding Chapel. No matter what kind of assurances Betsy had for me, I knew it was only going to be a matter of time before Mitch came back wanting to get back what was rightfully his.

And when he did come back, I was going to have to be ready for him.

Instead of driving all the way into base, I turned down Bartlett Avenue and drove a few blocks to the Hangar Inn. Back before I got married, I used to come here with the other crew chiefs when our shift ended. Strictly a beer joint due to some stupid local ordinance, the place was famous for its homemade pizza. However, the real reason why it was so popular with the guys on swing shift was that it was the only place open, and the owner, Barb Larson, would keep it open until morning.

When I pulled into the parking lot, there was only one other car at the far end. I recognized whom it belonged to immediately. A couple guys in the squadron said she was bartending there now. That was another reason why the Hangar Inn was so popular: Felicia Bianca Ramos Abellana.

First Mitch and now Felicia—I couldn't wait to see what fate had in store for me next.

I walked in out of the bright sunshine into the darkened room and stood at the door waiting for my eyes to adjust to the darkness. The familiar strains of "Hotel California" emitted from a jukebox to my left. The story of my life.

"Hey, stranger," a familiar voice said from behind the bar.

"Hi, Felicia," I said, walking in the direction of the voice.

When I reached the bar, Felicia leaned over and kissed me on the cheek. Her breath was hot and sweet. It might have been a beer joint, but Felicia loved her Jack and Cokes.

"How's married life treating you?"

She had cut her hair and lost some weight since the last time I saw her—right before Betsy and I got married.

"Don't ask."

"Poor baby, miss me already?" She laughed with a throaty, raspy laugh from years of smoking. Even though she had lived in the States for over ten years, she'd kept her accent. "What can I get for you?"

"Beer," I said, smiling.

"Mitch is in town," she said, pouring me a glass of Oly from the tap. "He was in here last night asking about you."

"News travels fast," I said, taking a sip of my beer.

"Hey babe, this is Adelanto. You know you can't keep any secrets here."

"I know. He's at the apartment now."

"He's *where*?"

"At the apartment."

"What does he want?"

"He didn't say."

The door opened, and two men entered. They looked at Felicia and me before they walked to the far end of the bar. I watched her sashay down the length of the bar and wait on the two men. She still filled out a pair of tight jeans better than women half her age. She had a few miles on her now, but she looked just as good and hot as she did the night I met her at the Airman's Club my first week at the air base a little over a year ago.

That night was also the first time I saw Mitch.

Felicia returned to my end of the bar and pulled up a stool. She leaned over close enough for me to smell her perfume and see that she wasn't wearing a bra.

"Be careful," she said, sipping a bottle of mineral water. "There's no telling what he'll do."

"I can take care of him," I said, staring into Felicia's dark eyes.

"If things ever go south, you still got my number, right?"

*   *   *

When I arrived back at the apartment two hours later, his truck was still in the driveway. I saw Betsy peering out the living room window as I neared the front door of the apartment. Calling the shack we lived in an apartment was an overstatement. Back during World War II, the Army Air Corps bought out all these chicken ranches with their long buildings and converted them into temporary barracks. Supposedly they were supposed to have been torn down after the war, but they were converted into low-rent apartments. Nearly fifty years later, these same buildings, with some improvements over the years, were still standing, and some slumlord rented them out to guys like me who couldn't get base housing.

Before I reached the door, Mitch and Betsy walked out. Mitch had an arm around Betsy's shoulder.

"Mitch wants to talk to you. I'm going into town to see Kimberly." Betsy walked past me toward the Toyota. "There's some pizza in the icebox."

Mitch laughed.

I started to move back to the car, but Betsy had already started it up and put it in gear.

"Don't wait up for me if you're tired." She checked her makeup in the rearview mirror.

Betsy backed the car up and spun the tires in the sand before she tore out onto the blacktop road. Mitch and I both watched the car move down the road until we couldn't see it anymore.

"You're one lucky dude. Can't say that I envy you, though. I had my chance. He rocked back on his heels, gazing up into the sky. "Sweetest piece of ass I ever had."

"Excuse me?"

Mitch moved past me, kicking up some sand as he moved toward his truck. From the back, he pulled out a cooler. "Didn't want Betsy to know I had this. She used to get really bent out of shape with my drinking. I don't think I could have gone another minute without a cold one. Beer?"

"Listen, Mitch, if it's about—"

"You know why I'm here." He pulled out a dripping bottle of Budweiser, opened it on the lip of the truck's rust-flecked bumper and hoisted it to his lips. Beer streamed out the corner of his mouth, and he wiped it away with the back of his hand. "It's a hot one today. I don't know how you two can still live in this place. I figured you for base housing, being an E-5 and all. Betsy probably told you that I was redlined for promotion a couple of times because of my drinking. No promotion. No base housing. That sucked."

Mitch emptied the bottle. He pulled out another. I moved out of the sun to a picnic table shaded by one of the few trees we had on our lot. Mitch followed, dragging the cooler across the sand and wisps of brown grass.

"You sure you don't want a beer? I figured you for a beer man."

I nodded and leaned back against the table. Mitch opened the bottle with the edge of his belt buckle and handed it to me.

"I'm not here to cause trouble. That's what I told Betsy. I'm not about to pull any shit. Those days are gone." He took a long drink and wiped his mouth again. "I'm not going to fuck with you, if you know what I mean."

"That's good to know."

"Uh-huh," Mitch grunted, sticking a cigarette in his mouth. "What's done is done, as my old man used to say. You can't go back and unscrew the pooch."

As much as I despised hanging out with Betsy's ex, I had to hand it to him—he was a colorful character. If things had been different, we might have been the best of buds. After all, our taste in women was the same. An F-4 screamed overhead. Mitch shaded his eyes with one hand as he looked up at the fighter streaking toward the base.

"What do you want to talk about, Mitch?"

Mitch followed the fighter as it circled over the base before it began its final approach.

"Yeah, I'm glad I don't have to fuck with them anymore." He turned toward me. "I only want what's mine."

Here it comes.

He chugged the rest of the beer and tossed the bottle into the desert. It hit a rock and shattered into brown shards. He grabbed another one from the cooler. He wiped off the water with one quick move and popped it open.

"What?"

"Come on, do I have to spell out everything for you, Sarge? You and I both know it was wrong."

"Mitch, I don't know what you're talking about."

"Five thousand dollars. Does that refresh your memory?" Mitch stared at me with hooded eyes.

"What five thousand dollars?"

"You know goddamn *what* five thousand dollars."

Mitch took another drink. The veins on his neck tightened. "I was sending Betsy most of my paycheck every month to put in our savings account. Turns out, while I was sweating off my ass in PI, she's sweet-talking some grease-ball attorney in Tijuana and all the while cashing the checks. Like I said, I only want what's mine."

"Mitch, I really don't know what to tell you. Betsy never told me about any money. It seems that this is something you and Betsy have to work out."

Mitch leaned back and laughed. "Something Betsy and I have to work out? Yeah, ain't that a fucking joke."

"Wasn't that why you came back here? Doesn't she know?"

"What do you mean, she doesn't know? Of course she goddamn knows! She spent the goddamn money." He drank some more beer and pointed a bony finger at me. "From what I hear, you two were screwing around when I was still sending her the money."

"Honestly, Mitch, I didn't know anything about the money."

Mitch shook his head. "The way I see it, pal, you're just as responsible. Now, you don't want me to cause any trouble for you. E-5 and all. Might not look so good the next time you come up for promotion. And don't think for a moment I don't know about you and Felicia."

You had to bring her up, didn't you, Mitch? If he wanted to threaten me by bringing in Felicia, he was not as stupid as I thought. He knew that it would be hard to collect the money without a little leverage.

Mitch and I sat quietly for a few minutes watching dust devils spin across the baked ground. He had already gone through a six-pack and was working on another. Mitch took a drag off his cigarette and let the smoke curl into his nose. He turned around on the picnic table and craned his neck toward the back of the apartment.

"I see Betsy got rid of my snake cages."

I shrugged.

110

Mitch moved toward the back of the apartment, shaded by an emaciated tree. He surveyed the area and kicked a rock into the spot supposedly where his cages must have once stood. "I used to hunt for snakes. It drove Betsy up the fucking wall. I had over fifteen cages and twenty snakes." He stretched out his arms to show where he had placed the cages. "You wouldn't believe how many people are misinformed about snakes. Did you know that a person is nine times more likely to die from being struck by lightning than by dying from a venomous snake bite?"

"No, I didn't know that."

"It's true. Out of the approximately forty-five thousand reported snake bites each year in America only eight thousand of those are venomous, but only around twelve people die from them. Snakes are the most misunderstood and feared creature on the planet, but they have every right to be here as we do. People just need to learn how to coexist with them," Mitch said, lowering his arms. He pushed out his chest and threw his shoulders back, proud to have shared this information with me. "Have you ever seen a Mojave green?"

"No, but I was warned about them when I arrived here."

"Let me guess, some dickhead butter bar told you about them during orientation?"

"Yeah," I said grinning.

"You're damn right you watch out for the Mojave green! Meanest fucking snake I've ever come across." Mitch moved back to the table and swigged more of his beer; he rested one foot on the bench with one arm resting on his knee. "The Mojave green is a strange one. It's not like other rattlers. It packs a badass poison that goes right for the nervous system. That shit will fuck you up quick. I've only seen one in all my years of hunting for snakes. Sometimes it's hard to tell the difference between a Mojave green and a diamondback, but I found out once.

"I was walking in the desert one morning, not paying attention to where I was going; you know, just walking. Well, I tripped over a rock and fell down. Dumb fucking luck, I thought when I started to pick myself up because at first, when I saw it moving—it was no more than two or three feet long—I thought it was a diamondback. I've caught a few diamondbacks in the past, and you'd think I'd know my fucking snakes. But this snake had moved into the shadow of a Joshua tree and I couldn't tell, at least not yet.

"After I got up, I tossed a rock at it to move it back into the light. Didn't budge. So I tossed another rock at it. I know what you're thinking, I should have gotten the hell out of there, but it wasn't like I was scared or anything. The snake coiled. The color froze me. I stood in my tracks." Mitch took a drink and leaned forward. "The Mojave green is a nervous one." He shot out two fang-like fingers toward my face just inches from my nose. "A real quick striker!"

He jerked back his fingers and leaned back. "That fucker just sat there all coiled up and ready for some action, but I was already gone. *Hasta la* fucking bye-bye. You want another beer?"

"No."

Mitch tossed down his beer. He picked up the cooler and moved back to the truck. After he had set the cooler in the truck, he slipped on his sunglasses and climbed in. "I'll be in touch, dude."

I was in the apartment before Mitch backed out onto the road.

After I ate two slabs of the cold, rubbery pizza and washed them down with a can of pop, I walked out to a small metal storage shed behind our apartment. I had to move a lot of boxes, mostly Betsy's crap, until I came to my footlocker in the back. I opened it and took out a small wooden box, the size of a shoebox, from inside.

Back in the apartment, it was still too hot to sleep, so I took a shower. I ended up on the sofa with a towel around me, watching TV. The phone rang twice, but each time I didn't get up to answer it.

Around ten, the apartment finally cooled. I moved into the bedroom, slipped on a pair of shorts, and stretched out on the bed. A breeze blew in from the desert.

Half an hour later, Betsy pulled up.

She banged the screen door and cursed. I could tell by the way she walked that she was drunk. I heard her walk into the bedroom. I felt the mattress give as she reached across the bed to see whether I was awake.

"It's about the money, isn't it?" Her voice was sharp and abrupt. She thumped me on the shoulders with the palm of her hand. "It's the money, right?"

I smelled whiskey on her breath and the same cheap cologne Mitch wore.

She nudged me again, but I still didn't answer. However, when she started to move off the bed, I jerked my body around and grabbed her wrist. "It *is* the money."

I released my grip. She backed away and stumbled over the pile of clothes at the side of the bed. After I heard the door click shut and the TV come on, I got up and sat on the edge of the bed. I grabbed a cigarette from a crumpled pack of Marlboros and lit up. I took a deep drag off the cigarette and looked out the window. It was a full-moon night and I could see all the way to the base. You'd be surprised what you can see on a clear night like this one was. Everything crystal clear.

After I had finished the cigarette, I reached under the bed and slid out the small wooden box I had taken out of my footlocker earlier in the evening. I opened it slowly and took out my pistol. The polished nickel-plated barrel caught the moonlight as I held it in my hand. It felt cool, comforting, reassuring against my skin. I watched the vaporous whorls of my fingertips evaporate quickly.

Yeah, Betsy, I have secrets too.

I gently ran my hand over the barrel. I hoped the inside wasn't dirty.

Going after Sexton

Right on schedule, Sexton entered Makanda Java at 2:00, walked to the back of the shop where he plopped down on a dilapidated sofa that I should have thrown out years ago, and waited for me to join him with a pot of our house blend. Every afternoon for the past ten years, ever since I started running Carbondale's only coffeehouse, this had been our ritual, our routine. Friends since our freshman year at Southern Illinois University, both of us stayed after graduating and carved out a livelihood and settled in a routine that was nothing we'd ever imagined when we declared our majors.

This day, then, should have been no different than any other day.

While my afternoon help took care of the counter, I joined Sexton in the back. He poured himself a cup of coffee and stretched out his long legs on an ottoman which was equally worse for wear as the sofa. He held the cup up to his nose and savored the rich, full-bodied, aromatic blend before he took a sip. Satisfied, he set the cup down on a table next to the sofa and stuck a clove cigarette in his mouth.

"I'm leaving," he said matter-of-factly. "And this time I mean it."

Sexton. That was his legal name. He had it changed after he read this fantasy trilogy, *The Sexton Chronicles*, and liked the name of the main character. He had been to three World Fantasy Conventions, including the one in Nashville in 1987, where he actually met the author of the chronicles, David J. Steele; after the convention, that was all he talked about for weeks. Sexton was tall and thin, and if one got past his mohawk, he reminded one of Riff Raff from *The Rocky Horror Picture Show*. At Carbondale's nationally acclaimed Halloween celebration, everyone who saw Sexton thought he was Riff Raff when he was, of course, just Sexton.

I never forgot the first time I bumped into Sexton on the Southern Illinois University campus. He was walking out of the Student Center on his way to Faner Hall when he was verbally attacked by this traveling preacher who was speaking before a group of students in this free speech zone public forum area where anyone with a cause or an ax to grind could hop up on their proverbial soapboxes and speak to their heart's content without being subject to harassment by school officials. Earlier in the year, NORML (National Organization for the Reformation of Marijuana Laws) had hosted a marijuana smoke-in, and the university or local law enforcement officials weren't able to do anything—that is, until you'd left, when you were subject to arrest.

I was on a grassy knoll lounging in the sun with some classmates not paying any attention as the preacher, who was holding up a ten-foot flimsy wooden cross, drone on about the evils of drugs, alcohol, premarital sex, rock and roll, and homosexuality. I happened to look in the direction of the preacher just as Sexton walked by in all his punk and Riff Raff glory. The preacher took one look at him and unleashed his acerbic attack on the immoral behavior of today's youth.

"And here you see the consequences of drugs, alcohol, and rock and roll music," the preacher intoned, pointing a bony finger at Sexton as he passed. The preacher, dressed in black slacks, white shirt, and black tie, was just as tall and thin as Sexton. "Here you see a man, a homosexual no less, who has lost his way in the decadence of our time."

Sexton looked around wondering who the preacher was talking to when he suddenly realized, with all eyes on him, that the preacher had singled him out.

"What do you have to say for yourself, young man?" the preacher asked.

Sexton squinted in the bright sunlight and held up a hand in front of his forehead to block out the sun as he looked at the preacher. "Come again, Padre?"

"You sir, wear your homosexuality like a scarlet letter on your breast."

Sexton looked down at his shirt as if he had spilled ketchup or something on it. "What the—"

That's all it took. Later, Sexton couldn't remember charging at the preacher and breaking the cross, but he did remember all the students yelling and applauding as he continued on his way to Faner Hall.

"What is it this time?" I asked, pouring myself a cup of coffee. "Music? Your job? Lucy?"

"Well, now that you've mentioned the music scene, it's been all downhill since members of David and the Happenings, Riff Raff, and The Bras graduated and a lot of the old bars and clubs have closed or are under new management," Sexton said, grinning.

For the past three years, every month or so, Sexton would talk about how he was finally leaving, as he put it, "to make something out of my life before I depart this swirling mass of life forms." Sometimes it was job-related; other times it was his on-and-off again relationship with Lucy, or something more spiritual or philosophical, like the time he read *Zen and the Art of Motorcycle Maintenance* and decided that he needed to go on an extended road trip to find himself. (He got as far as St. Louis and turned around. His dog-eared copy of the book was still on the shelf of free books at the front of the shop.) The next day everything was back to normal. It had been two months since the last time Sexton said he was leaving, so he was due for another epiphany.

We had all talked about leaving at one time or another. Until I started to manage Makanda Java for Gary Morrow, I thought about leaving all the time. I spent four years majoring in partying with a minor in film; when it came time to look for a job after graduation, I took that film degree and put it to good use as the manager of ABC Liquors where I ended up staying until five years ago, when Gary approached me and asked if I wouldn't mind running what at the time had been the only coffeehouse in town—the only authentic coffeehouse now that three Starbucks had opened. He figured I spent so much time hanging out here when I wasn't working at the liquor store that I should run the coffeehouse for him. By then I had socked away enough money that when Gary put the shop up for sale due to health reasons, I was able to get a loan and buy him out.

"My mom's boyfriend is a prison guard up at Vandalia," Sexton explained. "He seems to think that he can get me a job teaching painting to the inmates."

"What's wrong with Electric Ink? I thought Javier wanted you to be his partner."

Sexton had studied painting and graphic design in school and was quite the artist with a couple exhibitions and an acceptance letter to attend a prestigious school on the East Coast. However, after he got his first tattoo, he thought he could do better. And he did. He spent two years training with Javier—one of the leading tattooists in Southern Illinois (legend had it he was trained by Sailor Jerry)—and shortly after that started working at Electric Ink. Sexton's work was superb. Everyone talked about how much better he was than Javier.

"This is family stuff," Sexton said, snubbing out the clove cigarette. "It's something that I have to do."

I furrowed my eyebrows. "You're serious, aren't you?"

Sexton nodded and got up from the chair. He walked over to the vintage Wurlitzer jukebox, which was one of the coffeehouse's more endearing items. Gary had it when he opened the shop and I couldn't bear to part with it when I took over. Back in the '70s and '80s, whenever a band played at one of the clubs in town—Hangar 9, T.J. McFly's, Airwaves, or The Club—if they had a 45 rpm disc, they would drop one off at the coffeehouse where it would end up on the jukebox. There was a whole history of indie rock, blues, country, punk, and new wave on that jukebox. Some folks, hungry for nostalgia, stopped in only to listen to what a 45 sounded like. It was always a sad day when one those discs finally gave out after years of bringing musical joy and had to be thrown out. It felt as if a part of the coffee shop had died.

Sexton punched in a letter and number combination. After the jukebox came to life with a medley of assorted clatter, mechanical grunts and groans, a scratchy cover of the 1962 Tornados classic, "Telstar," began to play.

117

"I wonder whatever became of The Jerks," Sexton mused about the band whose 45 was playing. There were a couple more pops than the last time I heard this particular single, but after all these years, it remained one of the better covers of the classic instrumental.

"Whatever becomes of any bar band?" I countered.

"The Jerks were not just any old bar band," Sexton said, pointing a finger at me for emphasis. "Did you know two of the members were in Buckacre?"

I pretended to feign interest even though I knew the story of both bands. I saw The Jerks a couple of times when they played at T.J. McFly's. They were a fun band. Sexton thought he had the market on nostalgia and music cornered, but I was a close second. "Yeah, I heard that somewhere."

Sexton came to life, the same way he had when he'd gone after the preacher. "Everyone said they were going to be the next Eagles after Glyn Johns produced their first album in 1976. Of course by then country rock was on the way out. All good things have to come to an end sooner or later."

Sexton's voice trailed off as he stood in front of the jukebox and listened to the song a few more seconds, lost in his philosophical waxing, before he plopped down in the chair again.

"Oh, one more thing," I said, picking up where he had left off in our conversation earlier.

"What's that?"

"Lose the mohawk and the make-up."

"Oh yeah, good idea," he said, smiling.

When Gary moved the coffee shop from Makanda, a sleepy artist community about fifteen miles south of town, to Carbondale in the mid-'60s, it soon thrived as a haven for art, communication, and theater majors from SIU as well as Vietnam War protesters, musicians, and local artists. He rented out an old restaurant on Illinois Avenue, more affectionately known as "the Strip" and not only sold coffee and tea, but also had exhibitions and screened avant-garde movies at night.

And for years it was the only place in town where one could enjoy coffees and teas from around the world while eating organically baked goods. And of course, some of the latest music, courtesy of the bands who played in town and dropped off one of their 45s.

The day after the preacher incident I ran into Sexton sitting outside Makanda Java on a tree stump in front of a wooden spool for electric power lines which had been turned on its side and converted into a table.

"You sure took care of that preacher yesterday," I said, standing in front of Sexton.

"I feel bad that I broke his cross," Sexton said, looking up from a copy of *The Sexton Chronicles* and checking me out. He nodded with approval when he noticed the Cramps T-shirt I was wearing underneath my leather jacket.

"That's a cross you'll have to bear."

Sexton looked up at me and smiled. "You live in Stevenson Arms, don't you?"

I nodded.

"Yeah, I've seen you around. You know Susan and Becky."

Susan and Becky were two art majors who lived in a second-floor apartment next to the coffeehouse. I nodded again.

"Cool."

Over the years, Sexton and I grew very tight. He'd act in my student films; I'd help him lug his installation art from his studio to one of the galleries on campus. While our friends came and left, we were the one constant. We shared the same interests in music, movies, politics (we were huge Paul Simon supporters in 1984), even girlfriends. One night at the Trench Bar (this after-hours "bar" some friends of ours had in the basement of the house where a lot of people would go to after the bars on the Strip closed) after I had broken up with my girlfriend, Lucy, so I could go out with Liz, Sexton asked me whether I would mind him dating Lucy. And just to show him that I was cool with it, I drove the two of them to Sexton's place at the end of the night. That was just the way we were.

The only time we ever had a falling-out in all the years we knew each other—though Sexton would be the first to disagree—was not long after I started managing the coffeehouse. This was before he started tattooing, when he was drifting from one thing to another. He thought that because we were friends and all, he would have carte blanche at the coffee shop to pursue his interests—including his side action, which was keeping our "friends" supplied with recreational drugs—and would have his run of the place the rest of the time, which meant crashing out there when his girlfriend kicked him out or a landlord evicted him.

I lost my temper and told him that a real friend wouldn't pull this kind of crap—not if they wanted to stay a friend. I had always looked up to him and admired his free-wheeling attitude, but it was the first time that I felt I might have been blindly following Sexton all these years.

The mail carrier dropped off a stack of mail, mostly bills, a letter claiming that I might have already won ten thousand dollars, and another letter from my landlord's attorney. I didn't have to open it to know what was inside. I tossed it aside and poured myself another cup of coffee.

"Bad news?" Sexton asked.

"Just another bill," I said, not wanting to go there, and quickly changed the subject. "What does Lucy have to say about all this?"

"Excuse me?" Sexton said.

"How does Lucy feel about your decision?" Despite their on-and-off-again relationship, they had been together for over ten years. That was uncharted territory for Sexton.

"I haven't told her exactly."

"What do you mean by *exactly*?"

"Well, not in so many words," Sexton said closing the book and putting it in his book bag.

"Which means?"

"No."

"You haven't told your girlfriend that you're leaving."

"I was wondering if you could do it for me."

I stared at Sexton with my mouth agape. Over the years Sexton had asked me to do some pretty strange favors for him, such as the time he asked me to stand in for him as best man at a mutual friend's wedding, which went really well because he forgot to give me the ring. Supposedly the drummer from Guns N' Roses was in town visiting a friend of a friend and in the market for a tattoo. After waiting for more than three hours at the tattoo shop for his friend and the drummer to show, Sexton hurried to the church across town and got there just as the bride was walking down the aisle. He still forgot the ring, though.

"Look at you," Sexton said laughing.

"What?"

"I had you going. I am going to miss winding you up."

"You bastard," I said, throwing a magazine at him.

"You know you love it."

"Then we're going to have to throw you one heck of a going-away party," I said. "I'm sure there are at least one or two guys from Shakespeare's Riot still hanging around who could put something together musically. I might even be able to convince some of the original members of David and the Happenings and Riff Raff to play a few tunes. They owe me big-time. We'll have it right here and if it gets too crowded, we'll move outside."

I started planning the party in my mind. Depending on how much time Sexton had, I'd see how many members of the old gang I could round up. There were a couple of friends living in Chicago. They could hop on the Amtrak—The City of New Orleans—and be here in the evening. We were going to have ourselves the kind of party that we used to have when we were back in school.

"No time."

"Why?"

"I leave today at 6:00."

I glanced at the clock. It was 4:00.

One night, Sexton and I were on our way home from a night of slam dancing at Airwaves—this underground club in the basement of ABC Liquors—when we bumped into our friend Todd Larson walking along Freeman Street toward Freeman Hall, an off-campus dormitory.

"What's up, Todd?"

"I'm leaving in the morning. You guys want to drink some beer with me?" He pulled out three cans of Foster's Lager from the deep pockets of his trench coat.

Sexton and I nodded. Not exactly our beer of choice, but we pulled up a piece of curb and popped open the Foster's. Sexton lit up a joint he had been saving for later.

"Leaving, huh?" I asked.

"My mom's sick, and there's no one to take care of her."

"Sorry to hear that," Sexton said.

"You'll be the last two guys I see from here," Todd said, taking a hit off the joint.

Todd was a regular at Makanda Java, and if we had done our math right, from all the stories he told us, Todd had been going to SIU on and off for the past fifteen years. He'd get close to graduating and then he would change his major. Supposedly, he had been one of the demonstrators that got gassed in the Green Mansion, this prominent and dilapidated house on West College Street, which found its way into the annals of Carbondale's urban legends. During an anti-war demonstration in 1970, some demonstrators—including Todd, who just happened to be visiting a friend and ended up taking part in the demonstration—took refuge in the house after National Guardsmen chased them from the campus and into town. A tear gas canister was lobbed inside, and the house caught on fire. Todd ended up staying and started his career at SIU. He was the smartest man I ever met— just didn't have a degree to show for all those years.

"Doesn't look like I'm going to graduate after all," Todd said, passing the joint to me. "And to think I was so close."

122

I laughed so hard I thought I was going to piss my pants. Sexton rolled on the damp ground and spilled most of his Foster's. Then Todd started laughing. Good thing the cops weren't patrolling the street at the time. We would have all been hauled in for drunk and disorderly conduct, public intoxication, and possession.

"It was fun while it lasted, but sooner or later we all have to move on," Todd said. "Death, sickness, divorce—all just life's off ramps for all the journeys we take. Some of us have more off ramps than others. But for every off ramp, there's always another on ramp. Perhaps we'll all meet again someday. In the meantime, to quote The Dead, 'what a long strange trip it's been.'"

"Far out, man," Sexton replied.

"Hey, give some more of that joint," I said.

When I glanced at the clock again, Sexton had just enough time to walk to the station three blocks away.

"The least I can do is walk you to the station," I said, walking out from behind the counter.

Sexton nodded, but before we could leave for the station, a group of students came in all wanting café lattes.

"It's not like I'm moving halfway across the country," Sexton added. "Vandalia is only two hours north of here."

"I know," I said hurrying to finish the order. Sexton would only be two hours away. We would be able to get together every weekend if we wanted. I wondered what there was to do in Vandalia. It wasn't like he was leaving forever.

"Sorry I couldn't give you a proper send-off or even walk you to the station."

"No sweat, man. Remember, I'm only two hours away."

We hugged, and then I watched him head up Illinois Avenue to the bus station.

Sexton was gone this time.

Business was slow again that night. It was getting harder and harder to compete with the new Starbucks in town. I was barely making enough to cover my overhead and expenses, and the landlord was threatening to raise the rent again. I knew that it was only a matter of time before I would have to make a decision.

Up and down Illinois Avenue, the Strip came alive as students headed toward their favorite watering holes, cafés, and clubs. I looked out the large plate-glass window as the neon sign hummed and buzzed. A group of girls stopped out front as if they were going to come inside but then continued their way toward the heart of the Strip. When I turned around and walked toward the counter, that's when I noticed Sexton had left a copy of *The Sexton Chronicles* on a table near the door. There was no way that he would have left a copy of it here if he didn't want me to have it. He wasn't the sentimental type. Still, there was hope. I opened it to the first page, hoping that Sexton had written something inside, but it was blank.

About the Author

Jeffrey Miller has spent over two decades in Asia as a university lecturer, language instructor, and writer, including a six-year stint as a feature writer for *The Korea Times*, South Korea's oldest English-language newspaper. Originally from LaSalle, Illinois, he relocated to South Korea in 1990 where he nurtured a love for spicy Korean food, Buddhist temples, and East Asian history.

He is the author of eight books including *War Remains, Ice Cream Headache, When A Hard Rain Falls*, and *The Panama Affair*.

He currently resides in Daejeon with his wife Chiu, and four children, Bia, Jeremy Aaron, Joseph, and Angelina. If he's not working, writing, or reading, he's usually chasing little kids around his home.

www.ingramcontent.com/pod-product-compliance
Lightning Source LLC
Chambersburg PA
CBHW050802250626
47155CB00005B/2180